Ancient Lovers Never Forget

Arlene Michel Rich

2015

Publishing Division of

The Spiritual Awakening, LLC

Also By Arlene Michel Rich

Memoir of a Medium ~

A Bridge to the Other Side

2013

Awakening Your Psychic Power ~

A Medium's Guide

2015

Cover art by Seth Ruggles Hiler

Acknowledgements

To my husband Jim whose love and support, strength of character and sense of humor I have been Blessed to have as my partner in this life!

~and~

To my family and friends who keep me grounded when I need to be and help me fly when I need to soar. You have been an important thread in the fabric of my life and I am grateful for each of you.

~and~

To all the many Souls who have traveled with me through time. I am grateful for all the love we have shared and the many lessons I have learned.

Ancient Lovers Never Forget

By Arlene Michel Rich

Introduction

As I was writing my last book I was "led" to write a fictional book which has wonderful characters. My hope is this unique sensual story will capture your heart, make you laugh, cry, and fall in love with the characters as much as I have.

This love story spans centuries, worlds, and souls. It has many twists and turns which will keep you intrigued as to how it will all turn out. The title says it all, "Ancient Lovers Never Forget".

This will be the first book in my Destiny of Lovers series.

Arlene Michel Rich

CHAPTER 1

Do you remember the exact moment in time when your life changed dramatically because of a chance encounter? Actually, since I do not believe in coincidences it was destiny that we met on that hot July evening. I was the guest speaker at a woman's conference. Sharon, my contact person, had met me at the door of the hotel to walk me back to the room I would be presenting in. As she and I turned the corner, there she was. My heart stood still. As we got closer Sharon introduced us. Logan reached out her hand looking me straight in the eyes and I was mesmerized by her hypnotic gaze. I reached out to shake her hand and with that Logan pulled me close and kissed me full on the lips with such passion that had she not been holding me so tightly I surely would have fallen over. As I felt her start to pull away I reached out with my tongue and found hers willingly. My heart felt as if it was going to fly from my chest. My lower regions were pulsing. Each cell in my body had been awakened. After what seemed like an eternity I pulled away when I heard my host Sharon gasp. She exclaimed, "Well, obviously you two know each other very well!"

Logan's eyes never left mine as she took a step to my side and said with a smirk on her face, "I've been waiting centuries to do that again. Till next time!" As I stood there watching her leave I felt a part of my soul had been reawakened. Though I had not had the pleasure of meeting this beautiful woman before today, somewhere in the depths of my soul I knew her. As I watched her stride away with that sway of her blonde wavy shoulder length hair she turned giving me a final wink. It was like a shot of electricity was sent through the air straight to my heart. I swear I could hear an audible snap as it reached me.

A part of me wanted to run after her and just hold her in my arms. I had so many questions and if I didn't have hundreds of people in a hall waiting to hear me speak about ghosts and the paranormal I would have done just that. Logan's parting comment "till next time" gave me hope there would be a next time.

The next few hours flew by in a haze. I gave my lecture to a packed auditorium, stayed after to sign my books and answer questions and take numerous photos. I often think if I were to look at my eyes in one of those photos who would I see staring back? I know my mind was on Logan and how soon I could see her. How was I going to find her? She hadn't left me with any information at all. The only thing I did know was her kiss left me reeling and wanting more, oh much more!

I asked Sharon what Logan's last name was and how I could get in touch with her. Although she didn't ask any questions, she was clearly gob-smacked that I didn't know it after she witnessed that arduous kiss. She said that Logan had approached her early in the day to make sure I would be presenting my lecture in that specific hall but she had only said her first name. Obviously there was no mistaking Logan was waiting for me and wanted to meet me before anyone else would get there. If I was an artist I could draw her picture it was now ingrained in my mind. She had been wearing a white frilly blouse that just gently hugged her shoulders. Her long brown skirt came mid-calf on her cream colored legs. She wore a long gold chain with an Egyptian ankh on it. I had noticed it when she shook my hand and drew me in. It gently popped out from between her ample bosom. I noticed she wore a gold band ring with a carnelian stone on her right hand. I hadn't noticed if she had anything on her left hand. But her smile when she winked at me was most mesmerizing with her beautiful hazel eyes and big dimples I could willingly drown in.

Sharon and some others who had set up this lecture wanted to take me to a late supper in a trendy Manhattan club but I really wasn't hungry for food. After some convincing I reluctantly agreed. A town car whisked us down Fifth Avenue to a trendy club in Soho. Of course Sharon had made the arrangements earlier so we didn't have to stand on that long, roped-off queue to get in. We were led into a cavernous secluded corner of the club. A band was playing and the music was familiar but not distinguishable with all the loud chatter of the other diners. I noticed the dark ornate oak bar had people three deep waiting to get a drink. It felt good to sit down and relax for a while and just notice my surroundings. Without ordering, a favorite drink of mine was placed in front of me. Glasses were raised and a toast was given on my behalf.

As the night wore on and the music got louder I realized I had not told anyone what my favorite drink was. That was very curious. Just then as I was about to ask Sharon how she had found out what my old time favorite drink was, another one was placed in front of me. I knew I had never written about it before. I felt her presence before she leaned over and whispered in my ear, "I hope I remembered your drink correctly." As I turned my head in the direction of the whisper she kissed me. It was sweet with a need that was just below the surface. As she pulled away she said there was much more waiting for me if I wanted and I should meet her outside in twenty minutes. The whole exchange happened so quickly that I wasn't sure I hadn't dreamt it. No one at the table seemed to have noticed or if they did they were too polite to ask questions. Twenty minutes seemed like an eternity to have to wait. I looked at my companions and decided they would not miss me if I left. Everyone was deep in conversation or at least they were doing their best to communicate across the expanse of the huge table with the music growing louder as the night wore on. I took a few sips of my drink. Yes it was definitely the one I had made up years ago when I had attended a friends party.

I remember I had brought a magnum size bottle of red wine and when my date went to get me another glass they found the bottle was empty. I could hardly believe that because there was plenty of booze on the counter when we arrived. Most guests had brought some libations with them. Apparently, everyone enjoyed what I had brought best. Since it was very early on in that party I decided I'd make do with whatever drinks were left. Without much choice I decided to be a little adventurous and add a little of this to a little of that and voila! I had made my own delicious concoction! I remembered what I had put together at the party and bought all the ingredients to have at my flat. Whenever I felt like having something different I would mix up my own drink. I don't remember sharing the ingredients with anyone and certainly not the precise measure of each of them. All those many years ago I had poured into a pint-sized glass a 1/2 jigger of Don Jose Tequila, a 1/2 jigger of Smirnoff vodka, and a 1/2 jigger of Grand Mariner, which I finished off with 3 or 4 ounces of ginger ale and garnished with 1 slice of orange and 2 slices of lime. It was lovely! I called it the Devil's Kick. Logan had somehow known the ingredients right down to the 1 piece of orange and 2 piece of lime garnishment. Who was this mysterious sexy chick, and how did she know so much about me? I guess I would find out soon.

I stood up and stretched and went around the table saying my goodbyes and thanking Sharon for arranging a wonderful event for me. My book publicist had contacted all the various organizations I would be speaking at for my tour in the States. However, without efficient people like Sharon to have everything run so smashingly it could be rather dodgy. She said the limo would take me back to my hotel and that the driver already had the address and that he could come back and get them later. I told her that it wasn't necessary that I would just take a cab and to please write the name of the hotel on a piece of paper for me to give the cabbie. She efficiently whipped out the card with all the hotel information. I thanked her again and made my way to the restroom to freshen up.

As I stepped outside into the cool Manhattan air I was met by an incredible big smile and swept into the waiting arms of Logan. The kiss this time was long and arduous and promised a lot more to come. When I looked up the limo driver appeared and came around opening the back door for us. I took one look at Logan and without a word she nodded and stepped into the waiting limo. When I got in behind her I asked where to and she said, "Your place or mine?" I thankfully pulled out the card with the hotel's information on it and when Logan saw the name she took it from my hand and gave it to the driver. Within minutes we were downtown through Central Park and once again the driver opened the door for us. When I approached The Plaza's ornate front desk and told them who I was, the receptionist said that my bags had been brought up earlier and that the bar was fully stocked. She also informed me that there would be complimentary light snacks sent up shortly and asked if there was anything else that I needed. I replied nothing that I could think of but I would let her know.

I turned and saw that Logan had taken a seat on one of the upholstered chairs in the lobby. I noticed all the men and some of the women were eyeing her up and down. She wasn't what I would call a knockout but she exuded sensuality. Just then she noticed I too was undressing her with my eyes and she stood and walked straight towards me with open arms and practically leapt into my arms with a wet kiss placed firmly on my lips. I was a little taken back by this. She obviously did not care where we were or what people may think. I on the other hand was not as comfortable with such open public displays of affection. I guess I stiffened and she released me and I led her to the lift. I thought she may attack me once inside it, however she controlled herself and kept her distance in front of the two other people in the lift with us. I did notice the guy was gently rubbing his date's rear end as he nuzzled her neck. The young woman he had with him seemed unfazed by his amorous behavior. I would have said get a room but obviously they had that under control. Just then, Logan looked at me from behind where the couple were standing and she mockingly ran her own hands over her body and made kissing motions. I cracked up. She definitely knew how to diffuse the situation and get me to lighten up. After all it was a beautiful Saturday night in a wonderful American city and we were on our way up to what would probably be a gorgeous suite. Just then my mind said Stop! What the hell was I doing?! I was on the way up to a hotel room alone with a woman I just met a few hours ago! I know my body wanted to get to know all about Logan. I wanted to find out how she knew so much about me and why it was that when she kissed me I felt hypnotized, as if I was drifting in space with no sense of time.

The lift stopped just then and the other couple got out. Logan took the opportunity to come over to me and look me straight in the eyes as she said, "don't worry, all will be revealed to you in time!" The elevator doors opened on my floor and she skipped ahead of me looking over her shoulder with that impish grin. Am I that obvious that she knows what I am thinking or is she a psychic that reads my every thought? Whichever she was I really enjoyed watching her move. When I opened the door to my suite I was very impressed. I had heard about the famous New York Plaza Hotel but I wasn't expecting such spaciousness and grandeur. I went into the bedroom to see if my luggage had indeed arrived before me. I also wanted to check out the bedroom. Yes, a king size bed!

I returned to the living room a few minutes later and Logan had already fixed us both a drink. True to form it was my favorite drink exactly, right down to the orange and lime. Perfect! As she handed me my drink I started to ask her how she knew about the ingredients and she silenced me once again with a kiss. She put her finger to her lip and said, "Drink first, talk later." I actually felt I had done enough drinking earlier but sipped my drink now in obedience. Humph that thought struck a chord with me. I felt she was almost in charge of me, that I had to obey her commands. Where had that thought come from? Odd, indeed! I chose to sit on the chair opposite the comfy looking couch that Logan had sat down on. With a sly look she asked me if I didn't trust myself to be that close to her. Before I had a chance to say of course I could control myself around her she took off her shoes and tucked her feet under her thighs and her skirt hiked up.

"Is it hot in here?" I asked as I got up to wipe my brow and put the air conditioner on higher. Perhaps if she got a little chill she'd be inclined to cover up more. I had thoughts in my head of running my hands up her thighs and spreading.

"Oh, I'm sorry Logan were you asking me a question just then? I may have dozed off, jet lag perhaps!" I managed to blurt out. With that dazzling smile she gave me that look that said she knew exactly what I really had been thinking. Before I had a chance to let my mind go down that road again there was a knock at the door. I had completely forgotten that the hotel was sending up a light snack. When the hotel employee wheeled the trolley into my room he took one look at Logan and apologized for the interruption. I lied and said no worries he hadn't interrupted anything. I gave him a good tip and off he went smiling to himself. Just before I closed the door I think I heard him mumble under his breath that he'd know what to do with her.

Even though I had eaten supper earlier than usual, here in the states 6:00 pm was the usual time unless you were going to the theater, then you'd eat a light dinner and have something in a pub after the show. In England an early dinner is considered 8:00 pm. Speaking of England, I thought I might be able to ring home and check on the pups at that point. With the five hour time difference it would be morning in the UK. My friend Kiernan was graciously puppy sitting in my flat whilst I made my debut book tour in the states. I think Kiernan enjoyed sleeping in my bed much more than I'd care to think about. I know in the past when I've been abroad the sheets would all be changed when I arrived home but my pillows would have a scent I was not familiar with on them. No worries, so long as the pups were well taken care of, which they always seemed to be, it was ok by me.

As much as I wanted to find out everything there was to know about Logan I was really knackered. Once again as if reading my mind she looked at me and said, "Why don't we call it a night and get together tomorrow, or should I say later today." I looked at the clock and it was already half past two in the morning. I told her to let me call the desk and get her a taxi to take her home. She shyly lowered her eyes and said, "Or perhaps I can just stay? I see there is a lounging couch in the dressing area." I was so tired I said that it would be fine. With that Logan came over to me and kissed me goodnight. Since she had taken off those heels she leaned up to kiss me and as she did I saw the ankh around her neck, I instinctively reached out to touch it but before I did Logan grabbed my hand and said, "not yet my love, all will be revealed in time!" She guided me to my bedroom door where she gently, almost chastely, kissed me again and I turned and closed the door behind her. The transatlantic flight took its toll finally and I don't even remember getting undressed. I drifted off immediately.

I don't recall if I had set an alarm or if my internal clock woke me up but I did smell the delicious aroma of fresh brewed coffee. When you are someone like me who has traveled quite extensively for business, you get used to waking up in strange surroundings, but it takes a couple of minutes to reorient my thoughts as to where I actually am. Just before I remembered I was at the Plaza in New York City a soft voice called to me from the bedroom door. Had I had a hook up last evening? I didn't remember and besides wouldn't they still be in my bed if I'd shagged them? As my mind was searching my memory banks, Logan stepped through the door carrying a tray of coffee and croissants and fruit. I noticed that she was wearing a white dress shirt and nothing else. It was one of mine based on my personal design on the cuffs. As she laid the tray down by the side of the bed she leaned forward and confirmed my suspicion. Indeed that was all she was wearing at the moment. Technically, she was wearing that Ankh around her neck and a carnelian ring but absolutely nothing else except her "drive me crazy and back again" smile!

Without skipping a beat she filled me in on the previous nights activities which basically were PG rated. She had kept to her quarters in the dressing room on the lounging couch. As she noticed me looking down at my shirt - which she filled out so nicely in all the right places - she apologized for taking it without asking but she didn't want to sleep in the nude. Okay, let's erase that image before I don't wish to leave my bed chambers at all.

She clearly saw what I was thinking and removed herself from the edge of my bed and took a seat at the table she had placed the breakfast tray on. I excused myself for a few minutes to make my morning toiletries. I sat down at the table across from her and said, "Good morning Logan, did you manage to sleep well last evening?" Lame, lame, lame, I was thinking to myself, why didn't I say how gorgeous she looked? She smiled and said she had managed fine by herself. She poured me a cup of coffee and before I said I liked it on the dark side without too much cream and with only ½ teaspoon of sugar she made it exactly that way. Who was this mysterious creature and how did she know so much about me? As I looked at her again she took one of the chocolate strawberries in her mouth. She did not cut it first but started sucking and licking all the chocolate off the berry.

As I watched her devour only the chocolate and not eat the strawberry at all, it was as if we had been transported back in time. I had seen her do this many times before. Just then she looked up at my gawking stare and her face changed. It became younger and her hair was pulled back in a loose ponytail. It was long and brown with flecks of gold in it. She was no more than 13 years of age and I knew I loved her to the depths of my soul. She too was eating a strawberry in that same way. Her mother had made chocolate and we were in charge of dipping the strawberries and placing them on a waxed, covered tray for the guests that would be coming later that day. But each time Martha - that was her name then -

dipped the strawberry in she would lick all the chocolate off without eating the strawberry. She said strawberries gave her a rash all over her body and if she wanted to have some chocolate well, a few strawberries would have to suffer.

I watched the images fade and I heard Logan calling my name. She was clearly worried, I could hear it in her voice. The room was spinning for me and she suggested I lie back down in bed till the dizziness subsided. With her help I did just that. What had just happened to me, to us? Why did I see her as a young girl with a different name? I KNEW she was the same person in front of me and I felt I was the same person who was her friend helping her make chocolate covered strawberries in her mother's kitchen somewhere. Based upon the style of clothing we wore and the kitchen appliances, or lack thereof, it was sometime in the 1800's. The sugar nippers and marmalade cutter along with the wood burning stove were not of this era.

As I came back to present day and time she was shaking me by the shoulders and leaning over me in the bed. I realized she was not only worried but she was visibly shaken as well by what had just happened. I sat bolt upright in bed and as I did our lips touched and I could taste the chocolate on her breath. Once again I felt as if I was spiraling back in time. As I fell back on the bed pillow I grabbed the ankh Logan had around her neck. I heard a loud humming sound. An electric shock traveled up my arm, across my body and it felt as if I had been electrocuted. Logan cried out my name just before everything went black!

CHAPTER 2

Martha and I had taken the horses to go down to the meadow. We knew her mother's friends would be staying long into the night playing cards and telling each other the latest gossip. Martha's family were good, hard-working folk who owned the apothecary shop down on Fairfax Street. It had been in their family for generations. Martha worked alongside her father and older brother John. I worked just down the street at my family's general store. Sometimes when my father would send me to deliver a bundle of supplies to the men on the docks down by the river I would spot Martha sitting outside her family's shop. We had known each other our entire lives. Old Town was becoming a busy city with all the ships that would travel up the Potomac River from Norfolk. The river ran all the way out to the Atlantic Ocean. Some of my friends could hardly wait to be to be old enough to get a job on a ship and travel all over the world. I had no such fantasies. I wanted to have my feet firmly planted on solid ground. Actually, there was a piece of land my grandfather, my mother's father, had left me that I wanted to farm. I loved taking a tiny seed and seeing what the earth would provide after you tended carefully to it.

My father was not in favor of me doing this, In fact he said it was nonsense that I would even consider leaving the family business. The general store was the only one of its kind in the whole city and it had been in our family for decades. Whenever I mentioned tilling the fields he would get angry and tell me that it would be over his dead body that I would be able to do that.

When Martha and I got to the meadow we stopped and dismounted our horses. Even though I was pretty muscular from hauling all those sacks of flour and grain at the store, she was very agile and never needed my help. She came up to my shoulder in height and with her slim but well-toned figure she was pretty strong and independent like myself. I remember once when we first went riding she had met me at the land that was promised to me. When she came alongside my horse I dismounted and then went to hold the reigns of her horse and put my hand on her thigh to help her get down. She slapped my hand away and said she was perfectly capable of doing it herself which she quickly proved. From that moment on I treated her like one of the boys and it suited us both. On this particular autumn day we set out to go to my property.

I had, over the years, collected bits of lumber from the mill down on Duke Street. With Martha's help

I had taken the wood from old crates from our store and put them together to build a lean to shed. This was at least a little protection on days and evenings when a storm approached. As we laid down on the golden grass we looked up to the sky and told each other what we saw in the clouds. The first thing I saw was a Pegasus horse. I had learned about it in one of the books we carried in the store. My father would always yell at me if he caught me in the storeroom reading when I was supposed to be counting the items we had on hand and writing down what we would need to order. We had an older gentleman, Mr. Pentagast who lived out by Montgomery Street. He ordered all kinds of peculiar books. I loved to look at the pictures and learn about things they hadn't taught us in our one room schoolhouse. Once I tried to sneak one of the books out to show Martha but my father caught me. I didn't sit well for a week. Mr. Pentagast was a retired professor. He sometimes taught up in Charlottesville at the University. One day, if I was lucky enough, I hoped to meet him. I'm sure with all the books he'd ordered from all over the world he must have a huge library of his own

Sometimes Martha and I would make up stories about places and what it would be like to live there. We both loved to make up stories of Egypt. We would talk about what it must have been like to be a pharaoh in charge of all those people.

Martha said she would not have wanted to be a pharaoh's wife because we read that they were allowed to have many. I didn't understand why a pharaoh would want more than one. They had all those servants to take care of the house and cook for them.

Martha said she would like to dance like the women in those flowing dresses. I said I would like to see the pyramids and go into the Valley of the Kings. I loved listening to her voice. It was soft and dreamy when she told me a story of a faraway place we would travel to together. I never told her this but at night sometimes she would be in my dreams. They felt so real that on more than one morning I awoke feeling that when I opened my eyes she would be there lying next to me. From the moment Martha and I met at the church picnic as little kids I had always felt very at ease with her. Many times when she would start to tell a funny story or talk about something that happened when she was growing up I could almost finish her sentence. As time went on that's exactly what both of us would do. Some of the grownups who were within earshot would comment by saying we were like an old married couple finishing one another's sentences.

The only married couple close to my age was my older sister Anne. She lived out west with her husband Grant, so we didn't see much of her anymore. He had a job with the railroad and needed to go out to Illinois. My parents would get very excited when a letter came from her. The three of us would sit after dinner and my mother would have that anxious look until my father ceremoniously got the crystal handled letter opener out of the secretary desk in the corner of the dining room. He would read the first line stating that all was well and my mother would let out the breath of air she had been holding in the whole time.

Martha would be sixteen next month and I knew I would marry her. Of course I still needed to ask her. My best friend Luke said that if I didn't ask her soon he would. He liked that when we were all together Martha would join in with the boys' conversations and not be in the corner with the girls who would just from time to time look in our direction and giggle. Martha was both funny and smart and I could easily picture building a proper house for us on the land my grandfather left. Other than holding hands after the barn dances we hadn't gotten to know each other as some of the boys told me I should. As a Quaker there were things we just didn't do. Not that I hadn't had thoughts about it but at our Sunday meetings the preacher impressed upon us the sacredness of the marriage bed. Emphasizing the word marriage. We needed to start courting in earnest my mother said. That meant making plans for the wedding and building a proper home. I would need to get her a ring as well. I'm sure Katherine, Martha's best friend, would enjoy making all those plans with her.

Although I would hardly call myself a romantic I did want to make it as special as possible for Martha when I proposed. It would be great if my mother could help me pick a wedding band and order it as soon as possible. I could plan a romantic picnic, again with my mother's help, and meet Martha at the stream alongside my property. That was the first place we ever kissed in earnest. I remember standing on the banks of the stream just daydreaming about how my farm would look once I planted the fields.

I had been absentmindedly tossing rocks in the stream making them dance across the top of the water as far as possible. I hadn't noticed anyone around me until I heard a voice call out, "Is that the best you can do?"

I was so startled I nearly fell into the stream. As I regained my balance I turned in the direction of the voice. There Martha stood with a big grin on her face. She knew how close I had come to winding up soaked in the stream. Actually, I did have a fleeting thought of tossing her in the stream. Perhaps then those wide dimples would stop grinning at me.

Instead I picked up a few rocks and challenged her to do better. She said if it was a challenge there should be a prize. I hadn't thought of that. I asked her what she wanted in the unlikely event she won. She held her hand to her chin and with that devilish grin she said, "A kiss!" That was fine by me. Actually I thought she was going to ask for some candy or something like that. I knew she loved the mint flavored chews we had in the jar by the front of the store. Several times when she had come in with her mother as a special treat she would be able to buy a penny's worth. I would count them out into the small paper bags we kept by the penny jars of candy.

Before I had a chance to say anything else she asked defiantly, "Well, what will you want if you should somehow beat me?" I told her the first thing I could think of, the necklace she wore around her neck. She drew her hand to her throat and screamed as if I had physically hit her.

"No!"

I was so startled by her reaction that I did stumble backwards and wound up in the stream. Instead of helping me she just stood there laughing. Well at least she wasn't yelling at me. Thankfully, although cool out, my clothes would dry soon enough. When I asked her why she yelled at me about a silly necklace she said she could never part with it and would not say anything more about it. Then I suggested she tell me what my prize should be when I beat her by skimming my rock further. Once again her hazel eyes had a mischievous twinkle and those dimples grew wider and she said "you may kiss me!"

Well that was what she wanted from me as her prize too. Girls, they just don't make any sense at all sometimes! At this point I was wet and growing tired of this cat and mouse game Martha was intent on playing with me. I just wanted to skim my rock the farthest and beat her. I took off my shirt and threw it over a hanging tree branch to dry faster. When I turned around Martha had taken her blouse off as well and was standing there in her undergarment. Now it was my turn to yell.

"No! What are you doing?" I asked.

She said she didn't want me to have an advantage by being unencumbered by a shirt. I just prayed no one else showed up. That poufy blouse she had on sure had covered up a lot! Maybe that was her ploy to make me think about her breasts and throw off my game. I wasn't about to let that happen. Too bad we weren't playing for her necklace. Now that she took her outer garment off I had a better view of the ornament that was on it. It was a metal cross like figure with a loop shape at the top. It seemed vaguely familiar. I was going to ask her what you called it but I didn't want to be yelled at again. I turned slightly away and said ladies first. She then proceeded to wiggle about the banks of the river bending down picking up a rock then straightening up and dropping it saying it wasn't the right one. This went on for ten or more minutes before I finally said for her to just pick one or she would automatically be the loser. With a defiant look on her face she leaned down and picked up the same rock she had just dropped and said, "Fine, be that way!"

With that she stood up straight and started spinning around in circles. As she did the ornament at the end of the necklace came out from between her breasts and as the fading sunlight shone upon it the rays from the sun changed its color. It changed from a golden metal to a deep purple. I was mesmerized by it. Martha then put her arms out straight from her waist and started spinning even faster. Her ponytail was standing straight out behind her as well. I couldn't take my eyes off her. Just as I was about to go over and stop her from spinning she threw the stone. It skimmed along the water to the other side of the stream where it landed somewhere on the other bank. WOW! That was incredible! How did that happen?

I never was able to get it half way across. Just then I looked back over towards Martha who had stopped spinning and was holding the ornament around her neck in her hand grinning at me. She said, in a matter-of-fact tone, "I win, now you may kiss me!" She was right about that. There was no way on earth I was going to throw mine anywhere near hers so I may as well concede. With that I took her in my arms determined to kiss that smirk off her face. The ornament that was hanging on the end of the necklace touched my skin and I felt like I had been branded by it. Though Martha's kiss was warm and tingly I moved away from her to look down at my chest. It scorched my skin and left a red mark in that strange shape it had. Instead of her apologizing to me for hurting me she exclaimed, "I knew you were the one, this proves it!" I didn't know if all that spinning she did had rattled her brain but I knew it hurt like hell and I needed to put a salve on it as soon as possible. As I started to put my shirt back on she came over to me and put both hands on my shoulders and leaned in and kissed where the mark had been made. When she did this I felt dizzy and weightless. I then had the thought to pull the chain off her neck and throw it in the river to cool. She shouldn't have it around her neck where it could burn her breasts. As I reached for it I heard a loud humming sound and an electric shock traveled up my arm, across my body and everything went black!

CHAPTER 3

Logan was slapping my face as I came to.

"Thank God, I thought you were leaving me again!"

As I slowly sat up in bed my head ached and I felt a severe pain on my chest, a burning sensation. Had I spilled coffee on myself when I passed out I thought. My cheeks hurt but that was probably from Logan slapping me. Who is this woman and why is this happening to me?

I felt I needed to get up and out of here this minute. Whatever just happened I wanted to shower and check out immediately. I could easily go a day in advance to my next lecture in Philadelphia and take advantage of the hotel spa. This woman had been nothing but weird since I met her and I felt a need to distance myself from her. Logan slowly backed out of the room saying she would wait for me to get dressed in the adjacent sitting room.

Although I felt wobbly I managed to get my clean clothes gathered and start a hot shower. As I disrobed I caught a glimpse of myself in the full length mirror.

"OH MY GOD!" I blurted out.

As I looked down at my chest there was a bright red mark about three inches long in the shape of an Egyptian ankh. Dear God, had that woman drugged me and then tattooed me? With the steam from the hot shower misting up the enormous room I hadn't noticed Logan slip into the room. She was still wearing my dress white shirt.

"Don't be afraid my love, let me explain!" she said as she tiptoed closer. I looked around for something I could use as a weapon; this woman was clearly crazy. First she stalks me at my event at the hotel and later shows up at the restaurant. Then she obviously spiked my drink, then branded me and now God only knows what she is capable of. I know she couldn't be hiding anything on her person, she was barefoot and clearly naked under my shirt. As she started to come near me I put my hand up and told her not to come any closer. She asked me to please stay calm and she would explain everything as best she could. I realized during this exchange that I was standing there completely naked. I was so shocked by the Ankh emblazoned on my chest that I could hardly think straight. As I looked back at Logan she was holding my robe that I had hung on the back of the door in her right hand. She had her left hand on the button of her shirt, or more correctly, my shirt. She had a smirk on her face that challenged me to choose. Was I to be given my robe to put on or her shirt off? Before I could decide my shirt dropped to the floor with my robe landing on top of it. There stood Logan, wearing nothing at all except the chain around her neck with the ankh!

She was so sexy! Her breasts were full and I wanted very much to reach out and touch them, with my hands, with my lips. My mind screamed "hold on!" This was a ploy for me to forget how she had drugged and maimed me. With one quick move Logan was in my arms and then she touched where the scar was, first with her hand then with her lips. As she kissed the scar it changed colors, first a brighter red than it had been a minute before, than a deep purple. When she did this I felt dizzy and weightless. As I reached out to grasp something to steady myself I touched the ankh around Logan's neck. I heard a loud humming sound and an electric shock traveled up my arm across my body and everything went black!

CHAPTER 4

I woke up shivering with Martha lying beside me sleeping. It was nightfall and the stars shone brightly above us. We were laying on the grass down by the stream on my property. My shirt was unbuttoned and damp. I started to rise up on my elbows and my movement woke her up. Her look was worried. I didn't know what time it was but judging from the sky I knew it was much later than we were expected to be back at our homes. She asked me how I was feeling. When I stood up I was a little woozy but that was probably just from being disoriented. I started to apologize for falling asleep on her. The last thing I remembered was challenging her to a rock throwing contest. I better start going to bed earlier and not stay up so late reading. I felt like I could sleep a lifetime now and it wouldn't be enough.

She stood also smoothing down her skirt and brushing the grasses off her clothing. Our horses were drinking from the stream. I said we had better skedaddle on home. I asked her if she wanted me to ride with her to explain to her parents why we were so late. That I had obviously fallen into a dead sleep and she couldn't wake me up and didn't want to leave me. She said no that she would be ok. Her parents trusted me to be a perfect gentleman.

We rode back in silence, just the sounds of the night larks and the horses treading through the tall golden grasses. Just before she would need to head south we pulled alongside each other's horses and I leaned over and kissed her goodnight. I told her I would stop at the apothecary to see her around noon and bring some cheese and a loaf of bread and a few bottles of pop. If she was allowed we could go down to the park and have a picnic. She said she would love that. As I rode the rest of the way alone I felt embarrassed that I had fallen asleep on Martha. I hope I didn't snore. Oh well, if I did she should get used to it if she is going to be my wife, I thought.

When I arrived home all the lights were out accept the one in the kitchen. The kerosene lantern was turned down very low and it threw a shadowy cloak of darkness in the corners of the room. I tiptoed over and turned it completely off. I had almost made it to my room when my parents' door squeaked and my mother peered out around the corner of the door. She whispered, "Is everything alright Matthew?" I told her it was and that I would explain in the morning. She asked if everything was good with Martha and I told her it was. She threw me a kiss and said goodnight.

It took me all of one second to get undressed and under the covers. I fell into a deep sleep. My dreams were jumbled, one minute I was with Martha down by the stream and the next we were in a big city setting. I had never been to a city but I imagined what it would be like from the letters my sister sent. She lived in Chicago and they had gone by train to various big cities. Martha's hair was a different color though in my dream. It was light blonde and she wore it loose over her shoulders. In my dreams it was almost as if I could taste her lips and feel our naked bodies next to one another. I woke up thinking that it was definitely time to propose and share a marriage bed. I would love waking up every morning looking at her beautiful face next to mine. The sooner the better.

The next morning when I went into the kitchen my mother asked me what had happened that I was so late getting in. I explained that I simply fell in a deep sleep and Martha couldn't wake me up and then she fell asleep as well. My mother gave me a sly look as if to say, "couldn't you come up with a better excuse?" I just ate my breakfast quickly and then told her how I planned to ask Martha to marry me soon. Once I told her I would want her help picking out a wedding band and some other details she got up from her chair so quickly to come give me a hug and kiss that the chair fell backwards with a thud.

Just then my father came into the room with a scowl on his face asking what all the noise was about. My mother promptly told him the exciting news. I didn't even have a chance to get a word in edgewise. He simply looked in my direction and said he hoped Martha would knock some sense into me about all this foolishness about being a farmer. As the only daughter of Mr. and Mrs. Stabler he knew they would want their daughter to be married to a man with a secure future. The Stabler family had owned the apothecary shop down on Fairfax Street for generations. I didn't want to start out my day with an argument so I just went into the pantry and placed a hunk of cheese and some fresh baked bread in one of my mother's red checkered napkins and took a bottle of pop and put them in my coat pocket. I gave my mother a peck on the cheek and left.

As I walked down the road to the shop I thought about how great it would be when I grew my own vegetables to sell at our store. I pictured having baskets flowing over with fresh produce. When people came to buy their grain and flour and jerky and so forth they could buy everything that I grew from my land. I needed to get busy building a home and a barn to keep all the seeds and equipment we would need to run the farm. As I thought of how wonderful my life would be with Martha by my side she spotted my approach and hopped off the front step and her face broke into a beautiful smile. I could get lost in those dimples they were so big. When she came up to me she asked what was I thinking just then, I looked so serene. I told her about my plans to work the farm side by side. She let out a laugh and then said, "Well, don't you think you should ask me to be your wife before we build our Serenity Farm?" Instead of picking up on her taunt for not asking her properly to marry her I picked her up and spun her around saying, "That's it! The name of our farm shall be Serenity Farm!"

I was so excited I decided to go into the apothecary shop right then and ask Mr. Stabler for his permission to marry his daughter. I told Martha to please wait for me down by the town square that I wanted to ask her a question. I kissed her chastely and got up my courage, slicked down my unruly brown wavy hair and when I saw Mrs. Stabler behind the counter I was so nervous my voice sounded like a bullfrog when I asked if I may talk with Mr. Stabler. She must have had some idea of why I was asking to speak with her husband and acting so nervous because she came out from behind the counter beaming and wrapped her arms around my neck. She whispered to me that it was okay to go on upstairs, Mr. Stabler was filling out some papers in his office. I had been to their home many times for Sunday dinner or just to help

Martha out with something. I knew the layout of their home well. I passed through the kitchen and down the hall past Martha's bedroom and then past her parents' bedroom.

As I approached the office door, Mr. Stabler turned and greeted me with a warm handshake. He pointed to the other chair for me to sit down. I was quite glad to sit because my legs felt like jelly. I opened my mouth to speak and once again only a croak of a sound came out. Mr. Stabler smiled and opened his desk drawer and pulled out two mason jars and put them on his desk. Then he reached behind him into a cabinet and took out a bottle of whiskey. He poured two fingers worth into one jar and handed it to me. Then he filled the other glass and raised it in the air. He had a twinkle in his eye as he said, "Are you here to ask for Martha's hand in marriage?"

"Yes Sir!" I blurted out.

He laughed out loud and clinked my jar with the whiskey and said, "Good it's about time. Drink up!" I did as I was told even though I didn't like the taste of whiskey. It burned my throat as it went down. Although I did like the taste of tobacco and often smoked my pipe I never developed a liking for liquor. The few times I had some with the men to celebrate one thing or another I didn't like how I felt the next day. Also I did not like to think I may lose control and act silly or get riled up for no good reason and pick a fight like some of the men do. Mr. Stabler asked me what my plans were and how I would take care of a wife and eventually children. I told him about the property that my grandpa left me and that my plan was to build a home there and make a farm. Unlike my father who hated the idea Mr. Stabler patted my back and said that was a fine plan and that he would help in any way he could. He stood up and said we should go tell Mrs. Stabler the happy news.

When we got back downstairs into the shop Mrs. Stabler was standing with a handkerchief up to her eyes. Mr. Stabler took one look at his wife and said out loud, "I guess you know why Matthew came up to speak with me then." His wife flew into his arms to hug him and then came over to me and did the same. Mrs. Stabler asked me where Martha had gone to. I told her and she said she would be sending word down to my parents to come to Sunday dinner to discuss the plans. I told her politely I needed to ask Martha for her hand in marriage first. Mr. Stabler laughed and said it was just like his wife Sally to get ahead of herself planning.

I shook his hand one more time and as I left the shop and stepped into the sun filled day everything seemed a lot brighter and crisper than when I had entered. I couldn't wait to see Martha and tell her how it went. As I walked down the cobblestone road I nearly skipped along I was feeling so light. I realized I smiled and greeted everyone I passed. Usually, I will nod or tip my hat to people I know but am shy with strangers. When I saw Martha sitting against the old sycamore tree in the center of the square I ran to her. As I got to within ten feet of her I took my hat off ceremoniously and tossed it high into the air and as I looked up to the height of it I yelled out "Martha Stabler will you marry me?" At which point my toe hit a covered over tree trunk and I landed unceremoniously at Martha's feet.

She took one look at me and said, "Good Lord you're drunk Matthew Beaufort, you'll have to ask me again when you've sobered up!" And with that she sashayed back towards her home.

Just then I felt something wet and sticky down towards my right thigh. At first I thought I must have fallen on something sharp and I was bleeding. I slowly sat up reached towards my thigh and realized it was my pocket area and happily smelled the pop I had brought for our picnic. The bottle had not broken but it had lost its top and was flowing all over the red checkered handkerchief with the now very flat bread and smashed cheese.

I started laughing out loud. Really laughing very loud. So much so that mothers whose children had been playing nearby now gathered them up saying, "don't look at him, come along children!" Which of course made me laugh even harder. I'm not sure what happened next or how long I lay there. I only know my friend Luke had me by one arm and John, Martha's brother, had me by the other. They were balancing me between them and were arguing about which of them I should have as my best man. My head felt really fuzzy and my mouth was so dry it wouldn't have allowed me to answer them even if I had been able to make a thought worthy of the effort it would take to speak it. I did hear John say that his father must have given me a taste of his special whiskey. Luke asked what made it special.

"My father gets his whiskey from Mr. Douglas's distillery and it is very strong, if you aren't used to drinking it will knock you off your feet!" John replied. Which I believe it did!

The next thing I knew we were at my home and they had carried me up the backstairs of the store to my bedroom at the end of the hall. My parents kept themselves scarce as I was unceremoniously plopped onto my bed. I had trouble picking my head up off my pillow. I felt like I wanted to do this but my head felt like it was made out of a lead cannon ball. It took me several tries before I was able to keep it straight atop my shoulders and open my eyes at the same time without a piercing feeling to the back of my skull erupting. I looked down at my clothes that were all discolored and wrinkled terribly. When I looked in the mirror I saw my scrappy refection. My hair stood out at all angles from my head. My beard was untamed as well. I would definitely have to clean up well before venturing downstairs into the general store. I would surely scare the customers away. Even Sarah, the woman my parents had hired to help out when my sister left, would be less than pleased by my appearance. Sarah had shown up one winter's night with just a satchel and a letter of introduction from her uncle James Monroe of Oak Hill, Virginia.

CHAPTER 5

The Monroe family had known our family for generations and Sarah had wished to find employment in a more populated town. In his letter to my father he said his niece was of an adventurous spirit and would need to have her reigns tightened at times. He thanked my father for taking her into his employ. Sarah was my sister's age which made her two years my senior. She was equal to me in height which made her tall for a girl. Her build was quite good and she knew how to persuade the customers to buy more than they intended to, which made it good to have her here. The older men would often ask for her specifically to wait on them. Sometimes I would notice that if one man was already being helped by Sarah and I asked if I could be of service they would say they were still thinking about what they needed. Miraculously as soon as Sarah was finished they would remember what they needed her help with.

When she came to live with us, my mother made a room in the back of the store for her; she did not want to have my sister's old room upstairs. She wanted to remain on the main level where she could come and go without disturbing the family. My friend Luke would tease me saying she would be my live-in girlfriend and that I was a lucky man.

What Luke seemed to forget was that I was fond of Martha. Even still, whenever he saw me talking with Sarah outside of the general store he would roll his eyes and make kissing motions. What a dolt he could be at times. I told him if he thought she was so good he should ask her out. Luke would just laugh and say that she wouldn't give him a second glance with me around. Perhaps after Martha and I marry he'll get the nerve up to ask her. Even though she would sometimes have gentleman callers, as my mother would say, none of them ever came back twice. I heard my father whisper to my mother one evening after one of these men left rejected, that Sarah was just going to have to be less picky or she would wind up an old maid. After all she was going to be 21 in June.

Something I had never told anyone else was that one night two years ago, when it was sweltering in my room I went downstairs to get something out of the icebox to drink. As I came down the backstairs Sarah's door was open and she was laying in her bed without a stitch of clothes on. Rather than run past her doorway I stopped just past it where I could be unseen by her but clearly steal another glance. I had never seen a woman naked before. Of course I'd noticed women who had big breasts in paintings but I had never seen them in person. Sarah had her right knee up slightly and her other leg flat, between her legs was a mound of brown hair. As I looked up and down her lean body I felt my britches become tighter. Just then she stirred and I ran out the back door forgetting about the drink. I was halfway down the lane when I realized I didn't have a shirt on and my feet were bare. The hard cobblestones felt cool on my feet. I found myself in front of the church and had I been properly dressed I would have gone in and said a prayer to ask for forgiveness. I didn't think it was right of me to stare at a woman's body that is not my wife's.

When I returned to the house I went in the backdoor with the intention of running past Sarah' door. Instead as I quietly unlatched the back door and crept into the foyer I was greeted by Sarah. She was standing there in a long silky white robe with red roses on it. I noticed it was not completely closed around her body. Just below the belt near her waist area was a gap. I tried really hard not to have my eyes be drawn there but it was impossible to do. As I stood there gaping at her she reached out and pulled me into her room. She leaned close to my ear and whispered, "Do you see anything you'd like to touch?"

My mind answered everything, but instead I looked in her eyes and I shook my head no. Still, I couldn't help my body from answering yes! She reached up with both hands to stop my head from moving back and forth and planted a wet kiss on my lips. She then reached down to the front of my jeans and grabbed me and said, "You may shake your head no but this tells me yes."

She then took my left hand from my side and brought it up to her breast moving it back and forth over the silky fabric. As I did this I could feel her nipple change from smooth to pert. She asked me if I wanted to feel inside her robe. Once again I shook my head no and this time she tightened her grip on my crotch with her right hand and she kissed me harder. My right hand had naturally found the curve of her bottom as she leaned her body closer to mine. With my left hand I reached up to grab the back of her head and put my hand through her beautiful head of hair. She still had it up in pins and one by one I took them out to release it. I hadn't ever realized just how long it was. As it came undone I felt it flow past my right hand.

Neither one of us had shut the door yet, Sarah moved away from me to close it. As she turned she motioned for me to sit on the chair that was in the corner of her room. She took the two steps towards me and stood before me with an almost defiant look on her face. She leaned down and whispered in my ear, "would you like to unwrap your present?" I asked her what present and with that she took my left hand and brought it to her robes belt and said, "Me!" When she had leaned over, her right breast had been exposed and I wanted to reach out and touch it in the worst way. She must have read my mind because just then she took my hand and brought it up to touch it. It was so smooth and soft and warm to the touch. Then she stood up and as she did I reached out and undid her robe. I reached up to her shoulders and slowly revealed every inch of Sarah's body as the robe slid to the floor. Sarah reached behind my back with her right arm and leaned over and sat on my lap sideways. Now her breast was up against my chest and I could feel her heart beating. She leaned in and kissed me. As she did her lips parted and soon I was exploring her mouth with my tongue. I had naturally placed my right hand on her thigh when she sat down and as she kissed me I felt my hand moving up and down it. The more passionate the kisses became the more I stroked her thigh till I felt myself wanting to spread her legs and feel that mound of hair between them. Once again Sarah took matters into her own hands, so to speak, and opened her legs to allow me access. I slowly inched my way along her inner thigh and when I came to her mound I could feel the heat there. I opened her with my fingers gently and she tossed her head back and she cried out just then. I kissed her again more ardently and felt a sweet liquid on my fingers as I explored her more deeply. She took her breast and pressed it to my lips. I licked her nipple in circles till I pulled the whole of it into my mouth. Again she cried out and the liquid between her legs became moister. As I looked at her again I could see her eyes were glazed over in a dreamy way. She smiled and then stood up in front of me. She placed her fingers to her mouth in an expression to be quiet and then took a white handkerchief she had on her night table and placed it around my eyes. Were we going to play pin the tail on the donkey? Once again she whispered for me to be very quiet and to just allow whatever she was going to do to happen. She said if I felt like crying out with pleasure as she did to just grab the other handkerchief she had just placed in my hand and place it in my mouth. With my eyes covered I had no idea what was about to happen. I didn't want to not be able to see her luscious body but now I had no choice. It was with that thought that I felt her warm fingers on the top button of my jeans and I knew why she handed me that extra cloth. I promptly put it in my own mouth as I felt her slowly unbutton each button.

Deliberately, she undid each button and I felt her hand wrap around my manhood. She began to slowly move up and down along it. I had done this same thing to myself but it felt unbelievable to have Sarah stroking me up and down faster and faster. Just when I thought I would spew my own liquid out she stopped moving her hand. I sighed into the handkerchief. Then I heard her readjust her position and then I felt a breeze on the tip of my manhood. Where had that breeze come from I thought. Then I felt her tongue touch me and I came off the chair which only made me drive my manhood into her mouth further. Sarah started to put me inside and then out of her mouth in a continuous motion. I thought I would die it felt so wickedly good. Then once again she stopped abruptly and I heard myself say no, please don't stop. Sarah had once again moved and this time she sat on my lap with her legs straddling mine and as she moved alongside the front of my body with hers she slid my manhood between that sweet mound of hers. She started riding me like a bronco back and forth. The chair started to hit the back of the wall but I really wasn't concerned about anything else on earth than this moment in time and how fantastic my body felt. Just then I felt my body explode inside her and I gasped. Thank goodness I had that handkerchief in my mouth because I had bit down on it so hard - had I cried out I would have woke the whole town up with it.

My body and Sarah's were covered in sweat. She removed my blindfold and I took the handkerchief out of my mouth. I grabbed her hair in my hand and kissed her like I had never kissed anyone before. There was a need behind it. I'm not sure if it was a need to kiss her with passion or gratitude or just to show her I was proud she made me a man. I never imagined even in my wildest dreams doing what we just did together. As the moments passed we kissed more slowly and just held onto one another. Then I felt my manhood relaxing and Sarah let go of me and stood before me in all her womanly beauty. I reached out for her once more. As she looked down at my lap she grinned and said, "Not so fast cowboy. Once is enough for now." I stood up and pulled her towards me once more and as I grew hard again I slid inside her. I leaned down and kissed her breast kneading the other with my hand. I started moving slowly than more quickly back and forth. In one swift motion Sarah lifted herself up wrapping her legs around my waist. This made me able to drive my manhood in her deeper and deeper until we both exploded. Sarah buried her face in my neck and I felt her nails scratch my back. My face was caught up in her flowing hair. After a few minutes I gently turned and placed her on her bed and lay next to her, spent. Every ounce of my energy was drained. I stroked her hair away from her face and took in the beauty of her body with my eyes. As we lay there the patterns of the curtains upon the wall became more pronounced, which meant the sun would be rising soon. I needed to get back to my room before my parents got up. My parting kiss to Sarah was slow and gentle. I put my jeans back on, took a last look at Sarah's gorgeous body and opened and closed her bedroom door as quietly as possible.

I tiptoed up the stairs a man.

That first night with Sarah was two years ago. Now that Martha was going to be my wife I needed to banish all thoughts of Sarah in that way.

CHAPTER 6

My first order of the day was to tell my parents I had asked Martha to marry me. As I made my way to the breakfast table my head was throbbing. What was in that whiskey Mr. Stabler had given me? My mother was whisking the eggs in a bowl as I entered the kitchen. I asked her to please not do it so loudly. She smiled and handed me a glass of liquid that she had put one egg white into. It tasted lemony and it was fizzing.

I drank it down in one chug. My mother said she also put a little powered sugar in to make it taste better but the main thing is it would make my hangover go away. I attempted to stand to give my mom a hug and thank her but the room swirled around me and my butt landed me right back down again. She told me to just go back to bed and sleep it off, and I should feel better in a few hours.

I wanted to explain about last night and to tell them the good news about me and Sarah. NO! Not Sarah, I meant Martha and I getting married. Come to think of it I don't remember Martha actually saying yes. Did I actually ask her, or did I just dream that part? The last thing I vaguely remembered was Martha walking away from me as I was prone on the grass in the park. Going back to bed sounded perfect. I made my way to my room and fell into bed once more.

As I opened my eyes adjusting to the bright sunlight coming into my window I realized I had slept a lot longer than I intended. The sun was directly overhead, so that meant it was around lunchtime. My father was not going to be too happy with me. I had missed all the daily duties associated with opening up the store. By now all the weekly orders would have had to have been bundled together and taken out back to the storage room. We had customers who only came to town once or twice a month and they needed all their usual goods ready to take back on the long trek to their homes. Oh boy, I was expecting to incur my father's wrath once again. As I walked down the well worn back stairs and into the store, instead I was greeted by warm smiles and congratulatory greetings from all the customers. Standing side by side smoking cigars were my father and Mr. Stabler. My mother came out from behind the counter chattering on about some fine lace that she and Mrs. Stabler had ordered for the wedding tables. It was as if a light bulb went off inside my head. It was real, I finally would be making a life together with Martha. My dream of building a home and farm was taking shape in my head when I noticed Sarah standing off to the side. She took one look at me and ran out the back door with her hands to her face, crying. Apparently not everyone was excited about my upcoming nuptials.

Thankfully everyone was focused on me and didn't see Sarah so upset. I would need to talk to her at some point but not now. I wanted to go find Martha. Mr. Stabler explained about the congratulatory whiskey last evening that had knocked me for a loop. I noticed that he and my father had shiny gleams in their eyes and there was a half drunk bottle just behind the counter. That would explain why I wasn't handed my head as soon as my father saw me.

All the chores were done and I made my goodbyes and went in search of Martha. Her father said she was holding down the fort at the apothecary store with her brother. When I made my way down the street I wasn't sure how Martha would be greeting me. Apparently I was quite drunk and her brother John and Luke had to carry me home last night. As I entered the store the bell above the door announced my arrival. I would have liked to sneak in and notice her mood before approaching her but it wasn't to be. I brushed off my slanted halo and went straight over to Martha and began blubbering my apologies the minute we made eye contact. Her first words were, "promise me you won't have any of my father's special whiskey on our wedding day!"

I told her I would be sure to keep that promise and with that her brother, who had just come into view, said, "Well Matthew, aren't you going to kiss your betrothed?" So I leaned over and gave her a quick kiss on the lips. Martha must have been feeling pretty feisty with all my groveling because she said, "I'm sure you can do much better than that! Luke has kissed me more passionately than that and we aren't engaged!"

Luke kissed Martha - when was this? I wanted to know. Just as things were getting a little more heated and serious, in walked Mr. and Mrs. Stabler, fresh from discussing the nuptials of our wedding. That is if there was going to be a wedding. I really did not like the idea of Martha kissing anyone much less my best friend Luke! When Mrs. Stabler asked Martha why we were arguing on such a joyous occasion Martha and I said nothing. You could have heard a pin drop it became so quiet. Neither one of us wanted to discuss kissing and faithfulness with her parents. Just when I was about to say that I would see her later that night and continue our discussion in private, John told them word for word what our argument was about. Mrs. Stabler looked at me first, then her daughter, and then her husband who looked back at the two of us shaking his head.

He then said, "whatever assignations either of you have had with other people before your engagement should lie buried and never to be spoken about ever again. You have now declared your love for one another and plan a life together. Let that be the thoughts that bind you together evermore. My first thought was that sounded like exactly what the preacher may say to us once we go set the marriage date. The second thought I had was I am going to punch Luke's eyes out when I see him. And my third thought was to agree to this because than I would never have to tell Martha about Sarah. It's amazing how many thoughts came into my head simultaneously just now when last evening I could not form even one coherent thought. Martha looked at me and said she agreed to that as well. Whew, that was a close call! Then I kissed her full on the lips as if to say I'm the only man you'll ever kiss again like this, and I bid the Stabler family a good day as I retreated out the door.

As I walked south along Fairfax Street and east towards the river I knew I had some serious thinking to do. I would have loved to have gone to the property, I mean Serenity Farm, so I could draw some schematics of how my home and barn were to be laid out on it, but it would be too dark soon to see properly. Instead I went to the river where I always felt peaceful. Clearing my head in the saltwater fresh air was just what I needed right now. As I followed the river along the Strand I found a park bench to sit on and watch the boats as they meandered up and down the river. Sitting quietly, breathing in the scents and sounds around me I closed my eyes and soon my breathing became more rhythmic and settled and I fell into a peaceful dream state. I saw myself as an older man in his forties plowing the fields, my fields, and enjoying seeing the fruits of my labor. My crops were healthy and bountiful and I saw my home in the distance. It wasn't a huge home but it was plenty big for Martha and the children. Soon I would go inside where Martha would be preparing our evening meal. She was so beautiful; I loved her from the depths of my soul. She was everything I had wanted in a wife and mother to our children. Martha had stood by me when naysayers said I was crazy to farm the land after never being raised to do so. They said I should have stuck with running the general store or even gone to work with the Stabler family in the apothecary. Upon our wedding day Mr. Stabler handed me an official looking envelope that said...

"Matthew! Matthew! Wake up! We've been looking for you everywhere! You need to come quickly, it's your father!" Luke was shaking me awake. Disoriented from my dream I asked him to repeat what he had just said. He looked me straight in the eye and told me the doctor had been called because they thought my father had a heart attack. He was standing talking to my mother one minute and the next he was holding his chest complaining he couldn't breathe. Then down he went. When I realized this wasn't a dream I stood up and raced back to the store. There was a bevy of activity outside our store and as I approached, the people who had congregated on the front sidewalk parted as soon as they saw me. I caught a word or two as the gentlemen removed their hats. I heard one say, "at least James didn't suffer long."

I raced up the stairs to find my mother leaning across my father's body in their bed screaming, "No, it's not his time yet Lord, please don't take him" I looked at the doctor and he whispered in my ear that there wasn't anything he could do. He patted my shoulder and said those dreaded words I hoped I wouldn't hear. "He's gone. Your father is dead Matthew. I am so sorry for your loss."

With those words I fell to my knees at the foot of my parents' bed and sobbed more than I ever thought possible. I kept wanting this to still be part of my dream. Perhaps it was. Perhaps I would wake up on the park bench and go back home and my mother would be in the kitchen and my father would be in his usual chair at the head of the table and he would tell me to hurry and wash up that my mother was waiting dinner on me. I wouldn't care if he wanted to yell at or berate me again. I wouldn't care if he wanted to tell me how dumb my ideas were to become a farmer. I wouldn't mind if he told me for the hundred and seventh time to stop being a dreamer and be a man. I wanted him to open his eyes now and look at me and say he was alright it was just a mistake. Outside my head I heard this unmerciful cry, NO! To my horror I realized it was from me. It was true, my father was dead and I would never have a chance to show him the man I could be. A man he could be proud of. Just then I felt an arm wrap around my shoulders and the swish of skirt beside me. Martha laid her head next to mine on the sheets and wept as well. She wept for me. She wept for herself. She had known my father practically all her life and in a matter of hours he had become her future father-in-law and then her future husband's deceased father. I don't know how long each of us laid there holding on to my father's body but I heard a strong male voice start to recite a prayer and I automatically joined in. Somehow we all made our way down to the kitchen.

A church elder was there and asked when and where we would want to have a service for my father. Decisions would have to be made. I looked toward my mother for her decision, at which point the elder looked at me and said as head of the family now it was up to me. I heard my father's voice loud and clear in my head. "Be a man Matthew." I wasn't going to let him down. I took charge there and then. I organized it to be held at the Meeting House the following Tuesday. This would give my sister Anne and her husband Grant and the children, as well as those outside the community, time to make travel arrangements. I knew many of my father's customers would want to pay their respects. Those next days were a blur of activity. Although I thought we should close the shop people would still need to get supplies so Sarah offered to keep it open and Luke said he would be happy to help her. I agreed and I spent the following days with my mother and the church elders planning my father's tribute.

By the time my sister arrived everything was in place. I gladly left her in charge of my mother. It had been several years since we had seen one another and because I was so young when she left she kept circumventing my decisions. Finally, the morning of the funeral we solemnly walked into the meeting house. My father's casket had already been brought in the rear door and just a lace curtain was in front of it. The casket was closed, as is customary. A hymn was played and everyone stood as my sister and I were on each arm of my mother. With Grant and the children - my niece Emma and nephew James - in tow. As my fiancée, Martha followed behind us on the arm of her father and mother. Her brother John followed behind them. Once we were all seated in the pews, the elder stood and recited these words:

> *And this is the Comfort of the Good, that the grave cannot hold them, and that they live as soon as they die.*
> *For Death is no more than a turning of us over from time to eternity.*
> *Death, then, being the way and condition of Life, we cannot love to live, if we cannot bear to die.*
> *They that love beyond the World, cannot be separated by it.*
> *Death cannot kill what never dies.*
> *Nor can Spirits ever be divided that love and live in the same Divine Principle, the Root and Record of their Friendship.*
> *If Absence be not death, neither is theirs.*

A few people chose to stand and give tribute to my father. My mother stood briefly and said my father had been the only man she had ever loved and that she would mourn his loss till the good Lord took her to be with him again. My sister had chosen not to say anything. She had told me that what she had to say she had already said directly to our father over the years.

My nephew James was named after my father and was a handsome boy of nine. He went and stood near the casket and cleared his throat and painstakingly took a piece of folded paper from his pressed pants pocket. His sister, my little niece Emma, stood holding on to his shirt with tears streaming down her face. She was only 6 and probably not sure what was going on. He carefully opened it and then told about the army soldiers his grandpa had sent him and how he remembered grandpa teaching him how to fish when he went to visit them in Chicago. He laughed when he said grandpa kept calling it the ocean and James told him it was just a very big lake they were fishing in. My parents had only ventured out to visit them a few times over the years. Anne had come back with just the children a few times to see us. It was difficult for my parents to get away with all the responsibilities of running the general store.

The few times when they went all the way to Chicago, Mr. and Mrs. McPhee took over the store and all its duties and I did whatever I was told.

Just before my niece and nephew sat down Emma blurted out, "I love you Grandpa!" and ran back to her mother's arms. James stoically returned to sit next to his father. Now all eyes were on me. I had lain awake all night thinking of this moment and what I would say. If truth be told I don't think I really knew my father well at all. What could I say? That I feared him since I was no bigger than Emma. That I always looked for his approval but felt I rarely got it. Should I say how every time I was excited about something in my life and wanted to share it he was too busy working to listen? Or on the rare occasions at the dinner table when I did get the nerve up to speak to him he either would cut me off before I had a chance to finish my thoughts or he would laugh and say I was talking foolish? As I stood next to my father's casket I felt a strong arm come around me. Although I could not see anyone I absolutely felt a strong Angelic presence. This gave me the courage to speak from my heart and the memories of my father in his tender moments came flooding back.

The words spilled out from me in a torrent of emotions. At times I had everyone laughing with me as I remembered the time my father attempted to hang a banner outside our store. It was to commemorate the anniversary of our store. He had climbed up the ladder and it was my job to feed the banner to him. After climbing to the second story window he realized too late that the fabric was too short. He had leaned over so much that his foot came off the rung and he had nothing but the banner to hold on too. He looked like Tarzan swinging back and forth. When he did stop swinging it was because he fell through the window which was shut at the time. The crash and broken glass and expletives that were coming from my father's mouth had all the shopkeepers hurrying to the street. Fortunately, the only thing that was bruised badly was my father's pride. Later that day I walked out back to see my father standing by the fire pit. That particular banner was never going to be put up again.

Another time my father said that he would help me build a soap box car. I had waited patiently for weeks. Each night I would remind him the race was coming up soon and he would say, "not tonight I'm too tired." Without a moment to spare the night before I had found a couple of old tires and started to do my best, as an eight year old, to assemble my car. My father came out to the barn - probably to check on the horses - and found me covered in grime and sweat. He told me supper was ready and my mother was waiting for me. I asked if I could keep working and I would eat an apple or something later. He didn't reply he just turned and walked back to the house. The next thing I knew he came back with a picnic basket full of fried chicken and biscuits. He rolled up his sleeves and helped me assemble the rest of my car. Without his help I would not have been able to do it.

I realized at that moment of retelling the stories that I was a lot like my father. I was stubborn and thought I could do everything on my own and did not want anyone else's opinion. Although I did not win the race I felt good knowing he cared enough to help me. As I was finishing recalling times with my father the arm that was around my shoulder squeezed it and I heard my father's voice say, "I'm proud of you son!" The gulp that was in my throat would not allow me to say anything more. I sat down with my head in my hands and wept again in earnest.

I don't recall too much else of that day. My sister, Martha, and my mother kept busy in the kitchen with all the food preparations. The men gathered and drank a little whiskey out back. The children played hopscotch and jump rope. Each time I was offered a glass of whiskey I declined. I never wanted to feel that strange and out of control again.

CHAPTER 7

A week after the funeral my sister and her family traveled back to Chicago. I was sad to see them go. Martha and Anne had become close and had many conversations about our upcoming wedding. I had asked my brother-in-law Grant what I should do as far as the running of the store was concerned. Because of my father's sudden death, I really hadn't given it much thought. Grant had become a successful business man in his own right and I valued his insight.

I told him my plan was to start building a home and barn on my property and as soon as possible to get it up and running as a working farm. I would not have time to be back in town running the general store. I knew my mother and Sarah could do most of the day to day work but we would need to have men help with the heavy labor and receiving and delivering of goods to the waterfront. That was if Sarah was still even interested in staying on. Ever since the night I told my parents about asking Martha to marry me, Sarah and I had not had more than a few curt words between us. I think she remained civil to me only because of my mother's feeling. Every time I caught her looking in my direction it was as if there was pure hatred in those eyes. Eventually we would have to clear the air. Hopefully it would not end badly. I wanted the best for Sarah but she knew that my heart had always belonged to Martha.

Sarah was an incredible woman and I would always be grateful to her for showing me what it was to lay with a woman. Over the last year and a half we would get together any opportunity we could. After that very first time when I unexpectedly saw her naked and then later when she invited me into her room and eventually into her bed I looked forward to seeing her alone.

At the beginning I thought it would be very difficult to keep our meetings together a secret. When we would brush by each other in the store I would instantly picture her in my mind's eye as she had been the previous time we made love. I'm sure a hot flush would come to my cheeks as I know I had a definite bulge in my pants. After that initial night we spent making love in her room I felt it would be best to meet outside of the home. Just the thought of her doing those things with her tongue had me wanting to cry out in pleasure. During the day she would look at me across the counter and I knew what she was thinking. She would lick her lips and throw me kisses when no one was looking. One day however, she threw a kiss intended for me and Old Man Sullivan popped his head up from where he was looking in the case.

He said he thought the world of Miss Sarah as well and wasn't she nice to be making an old man feel special.

Later that same day we decided to meet at my property. Sarah had brought a blanket so we could lay under the sky with just the birds bearing witness to our passion. I could hardly get my own clothes off in time. I felt my manhood would burst out of my britches. I started to help Sarah undress as well and then she ordered me to just lay down and watch as she slowly disrobed. I was hard as a rock by the time she removed her panties and stepped out of them towards me. She was so beautiful with her blonde hair falling gracefully down over her back. I reached out to cup one of her breasts in my hand and she swatted it away as if I were a flea. She told me she was in control and I was to obey her every wish. So long as her wish involved me driving my manhood between her legs I was a willing puppet.

She knelt beside me and with one hand started to make circles over my own chest. Then she licked her finger and moved to my nipple continuing to make circles with her fingers. I groaned in pleasure. How did she know that would drive me crazy with desire? Then she leaned over, kissing my lips and then moving down my neck. When she got to my neck she started making noises and I felt as if it was a cross between being bitten and sucked at the same time. Again it made me hard as a rock. Then finally just when I thought she was going to lay on top of me or allow me to turn her over to lay beneath me she leaned on one elbow and started slowly stroking the inside of my thighs. Just when I would think she was going to grab me and bring me to eject my fluid she would stop abruptly changing where she would touch me. Sometimes she would lick her fingers and then gently touch the tip of my manhood. Circling the tip slowly. I couldn't help it I yelled out just then, "please let me be inside you!"

When I said that she had the biggest smirk on her face. She knew at that moment I was truly under her spell and would have done just about anything to be able to enter her. With the grin still etched upon her face she said, since you asked so politely, and she rolled on top of me spreading her legs so I could enter her. I grabbed hold of her buttocks and pushed into her as far as I could until she cried out and we both gave way to release.

When we were finished she rolled off me and lay by my side with her head on my forearm and her left leg over mine. We were intertwined and totally satisfied. Just then she shivered in the evening coolness and I grabbed a corner of the blanket to wrap around us. As I looked up at the night sky I was a happy man. The only thing I wished was to have done this with Martha. Martha was my true love. The woman who would be my wife and bear my children. I could never see Martha doing the things Sarah did to me. I could never picture Martha covering my eyes with her kerchief and putting my manhood in her mouth and licking it until I was ready to come. Once, when I asked Sarah how she knew what would drive me crazy she said it was simple, watch the farm animals, they did everything we did. To prove her point once when it was raining we ran to the lean to and when we got inside instead of her laying on the blanket and me spreading her legs to enter her she told me to wait while she turned away from me. She knelt facing away from me and told me to come behind her and enter from behind. I didn't want to do that, I felt I should be facing her. She looked over her shoulder and leaned forward with her forearms touching the blanket and opened her legs farther in invitation. At this point I was so hard I knelt behind her and entered her as she asked. I reached around and was able to cup both breasts in each hand as I drove my manhood deeper and deeper until she screamed my name. It was then that I realized we could never do this under my parents' roof again. We would certainly be found out by the cries of pleasure we had both come to release.

After each time spent with Sarah I would vow it to be my last. I wanted to focus on my dream of building a life with Martha.

But Sarah was like a drug I had become addicted too. My body craved her touch. Each night I went to bed thinking of what we had done and how my body responded to hers. Every morning I thought about how soon it would be till we could be alone together. The ache was a physical need and I didn't know if I could stop. Apparently Sarah must have felt the same because every time she was near me she would whisper in my ear, "When shall we meet again my love?" I had been totally honest that first time we had lain together. I told her that Martha was the woman I was going to marry. I told her I always knew Martha was meant to have my children and farm the land together. As wonderful as Sarah was I still could not see her raising children or working alongside me on the farm.

Luke and Mr. Stabler and several of my friends and neighbors met me the following Saturday to start work on raising my barn. I needed to build the barn before the house was done so I could set up my work space in order to build the house and start planting the fields. Within a matter of days the barn was raised and we had a celebration on the last evening. A big fire was set in the middle and the women supplied the food and drink. A few of the men had flasks that they would take a pull from but I had sworn off whiskey since the day I asked Martha to marry me.

Some of the men had brought their instruments and a dance was started. I looked at Martha across the campfire and put my hand out to her to join me in the first dance. She came into my arms and my heart leapt from my chest. Our dreams were taking shape. We were engaged to be married the following March, and our home would be built as soon as the land was tilled and ready to receive the first seeds. We were surrounded by the people who loved us and all was well in my world at that very moment. Of course I wished my father was there to see this. I believe even though he didn't want me to pursue a life as a farmer he would be proud of how well things were coming along. The general store was doing well, Sarah had agreed to stay on at my mother's urging and the McPhees agreed to help out as well. Mr. McPhee was a friend of my father's and he and his wife enjoyed working in the store. They had filled in many times for my parents so it was natural that they would help out now that my father was gone.

Unlike some widows who might have decided to wither and remove themselves from social gatherings, on the contrary, my mother blossomed. She became a social butterfly, joining the ladies auxiliary and started a woman's card-playing group. When my father was alive she spent all of her time at the store and in the evenings she would sit and read or knit while my father sat and read or whittled something. My father was not a man who liked to be around a lot of people, which is strange being that he owned a store which made it that he always had to interact with the customers. Perhaps because of that he chose to be solitary when he was able. I was very happy for my mother; she looked years younger now as well.

Martha was also a big help to my mother. They spent many evenings talking about the wedding. It was only a few months away and, according to them, there were a lot of things that needed to be done. I only knew that I had ordered a ring for Martha and that it would be arriving any day. I also had a suit of my father's that fit me so all I'd need to do would be to shave and trim my beard and make sure my hair wasn't its usual unruliness. I may have the barber trim it up for me so I'd look more presentable. My brown wavy hair touched my shoulders and on days when I was sweating I was able to tie it back to remain out of my eyes.

Loading, unloading, and hauling those long pieces of timber for the house at Serenity Farm was burdensome, but the house was coming together. I had all the sidewalls done and Luke and my friend

Jedidiah were coming next week to help me with the roof. In two weeks time it would be presentable for Martha to start fixing curtains and such for it. She and my mother had been busy planning and sewing things. I had asked Martha not to come to Serenity Farm until it was finished. I wanted to be able to surprise her with some things. I had made a bed for us that was currently in the barn. I also had made a table and chairs. Some of the elders from church had helped me with them and I would be eternally grateful. They were made sturdy and would be a welcome addition to our home. Any excess wood was stored in a pile outside the back door and would serve to start the hearth for cooking and heating in the fall and winter months. Nothing went to waste. The wood floors were all in and the ladder to the loft which would serve as future children's bedroom was almost finished. After putting in a full day's work I would arrive home in time to clean up, eat a light dinner, and go to bed only to rise the next day and do it all again. I was building muscles I didn't even know I had. I always had muscles in my arms from lifting bags of feed and flour and potatoes and such but my leg muscles were becoming bigger from climbing up and down the ladders. Some nights I was so bone tired that I merely took a blanket and laid down in the barn and slept there.

On one of these nights I decided to stay at Serenity Farm I had just taken off my shirt - that was filled with sawdust and sweat - when I heard the barn door swing open. I wasn't expecting anyone so I took the lantern over by the door to see who it was. There in the shadow stood Sarah. We had not spoken in months. I barely saw her and that was fine with me. I had enough on my plate with getting Serenity Farm up and running and building my home for Martha and myself.

Between the light cast on her face and body, and the moonlight behind her, I realized she was very scantily clad. I could see through the fabric she was wearing and the outline of her body made that old urge to want to bed her come alive within me. Without a word between us she came into my arms and kissed me fully on the lips, sending all resolve to the wind. Martha's face came into my mind just then and I pushed Sarah away from me and said, "No we cannot do this anymore." She looked as if I had bodily slapped her. She looked down at my crotch and said in a furious voice, "Your body betrays you Matthew, I don't care what your voice tells me, I know you want me!" That part was very true, I wanted to take her in my arms and carry her over to the blanket and do what I had done many times before. But that was before I had asked Martha to marry me. I was now engaged and the next time I was inside of a woman's body it would be my wife's, and I said as much out loud to Sarah just then. She stepped forward taking the lantern from my hand and placing it down on the ground. In one movement she leaned forward bent down grabbed the fabric of the thin garment she was wearing, and pulled it over her head removing it completely. She stood there naked with only the play of the flickering lantern illuminating her glorious body. The look on her face was defiant, daring me to send her away without partaking of the feast she was offering me. When she felt the hesitation she leaned closer and took my hand and placed it between her legs letting me know she was clearly ready to be entered. I could feel the heat and liquid and my own body responding. With every ounce of determination to remain true to Martha I pulled my hand away and stepped back. With a raspiness to my voice I asked her to leave. She then pointed out to me that I wasn't married yet and that no one would know. It had been over six months since I had made love to her and I was primed. With my lips and mind saying no, she was clearly right, my body was screaming yes!

She took this moment of hesitation to kneel down in front of me and in one swift well practiced motion, she had undone my jeans and her mouth was licking and sucking any and all resolve away. My mind exploded in all directions until the only thing left was this wonderful sensation. I grabbed

Sarah's head between my hands forcing her to move faster and faster. She was very accomplished at this and it wasn't long before I was about to spill my seed. I stepped out of my jeans and I pulled her up on her feet and kissed her as if my life depended upon it. This woman before me had my body totally consumed with her. I hurriedly swept her up in one motion carrying her to my makeshift bed on the hay and blanket. As I placed her down she opened to me and I drove hard inside her until we were both sweaty and spent. Her beautiful blonde hair was damp as I held her in my arms. I realized then that I would never be able to say no to Sarah completely.

She was my drug of choice and I was totally addicted to her. All she had to do was to offer herself and I was putty in her hands. We lay there together for hours upon end. Just when I thought it best she leave she started fondling me and of course I responded by becoming hard again. I started to spread her legs and just as I was about to go inside her again she pushed me off. She became shy almost and asked if I would do something different to please her. When I said I would do anything she instructed me to move my body down her body so her mound was in front of my face. She took her fingers and gently spread herself before me as she opened her legs wide. She told me to start by licking inside her as she had done to me. I was very hesitant at first and then I closed my eyes and let my senses take over. The more I licked her the warmer her body heat was and the more liquid of her own would erupt. I found myself diving in with gusto and taking little tiny nips with my teeth which made her cry out more with pleasure. She then asked me to move up to her breast and suckle them at the same time as I was fingering between her legs. She grabbed my hair and pulled my face till our lips touched and drove her tongue inside my mouth with such need that at that moment I realized I was as much a drug for her as she was to me. As we culminated our love making by her spreading her legs to me once again we fell asleep in each other's arms. It was the sound of a horse that brought me fully awake.

I hurriedly pulled on my jeans and told Sarah to cover herself and remain quiet, I would go see who it was. Serenity Farm was so far from town and anything else that unless you were lost it was your destination. As I came out of the barn door I saw Luke dismount his horse. He had tied it up to the post by where the beginnings of the house were. I presumed Sarah had tied her horse around back because I didn't see it. Luke called out to me and started to move towards the barn when I stopped him. He teased me that I must have had a long night working because I looked like I had just woke up. He said he had a couple of hours before he had to work at the docks so he thought he would come by and help me. Thinking fast I told him that I wasn't feeling well and that I had not gotten any sleep and that I was just going to take it very easy and he should go back to town. I thanked him for stopping by and told him we would still be on to work on the house on Saturday if he was still available. He said that he would be back again then. I stood by the barn door for a few minutes as he rode away. When I came back into the barn Sarah was standing in a back corner with the blanket wrapped around her. I realized just how truly flimsy her gown was because it was evident that she wasn't wearing anything under it now either. I asked her if she had any other clothes to wear home, she couldn't very well ride back to town like that. She told me she had a satchel on her horse with a change of clothes and toiletries. I told her I would be right back with it. When I came back into the barn with the satchel over my back Sarah was lying on the blanket facing me without a stitch of clothes on. Once again I was like a junkie needing my fix. I tore off my pants and obliged her willing body by driving my manhood into her one more time. In the last twelve hours we had made love of one sort of another four times. She was as ready and willing each time. Her need met mine exactly. I hardly could believe the things we did but it was wonderful. I helped her up slapping her on her bottom and telling her this time she really needed to get dressed. As she walked a little away from me she looked back over her shoulder at me and said to not excite her like that or we may have to go another round. She grabbed the riding whip that was hanging on the paddock and said playfully next time we can try some of that. I almost said there wouldn't be a next time but my body was already responding to the things I was imaging she might mean.

I made myself busy inside the barn as she dressed properly. She came into my arms once more and passionately kissed me goodbye. I walked her into the sunlight and held her horse as she mounted it effortlessly. As she rode back to town I realized I was in serious trouble with this woman. I had to give her up cold turkey or give up my dream of marrying Martha. I could not have both women in my life.

I went back into the barn and laid down in earnest to sleep. Even though it was the beginning of the day I was too tired to do any physical labor. My mind was so confused running back and forth between the two women in my life. I knew that Martha was a gentle woman whom everyone loved. She would make a great wife and a loving mother to all the children we would someday have. I knew

I loved her completely but I could not picture her doing the same kind of things Sarah and I did and certainly I could never picture her asking for me to do things to her as Sarah had. Sarah was obviously a woman who was not afraid of her own sexuality and not afraid to ask, or in some cases demand, what she wanted a man to do to her. My body obviously responded to everything she offered and wanted. Would Martha be as exciting in our marital bed? Sarah had said there were still things she could teach me and I admit I was more than anxious and willing to explore what those things may be. However, I was due to marry Martha in five weeks. The house would be finished this weekend and on Sunday I was planning on having a nice dinner for just the two of us here. Now, I didn't know how I could be in the same room as Sarah and not respond physically to her. If she and Martha were in the store or upstairs in our home together I would need to leave the room. What a mess I had created for myself. My last thought as I went to sleep was lying beside both Martha and Sarah.

As I fell into a deep sleep I imagined what it would be like to be with Martha on our wedding night. I had seen her without her blouse but not without her undergarment that time down by the river when we were throwing stones. I had fantasized about the night I would be able to remove all her clothing and set her ample breasts free for me to explore. Sarah had shown me ways to make a woman scream with desire and I fully intended to do this with my wife. Just as I was lying there in the darkened barn I felt lips kiss me. Rather than open my eyes I decided to just enjoy Sarah's lovely body once again. That woman was insatiable but I had rested long enough for my body to respond. I pulled her body on top of mine and parted her sweet lips with mine. I hadn't put my shirt back on and I could feel her clothing rubbing against my body. In what I hoped to be a swift move I deftly unbuttoned her blouse and slid my hand beneath her undergarment intending to caress her breast. Instead I felt the cold metal of something and as I opened my eyes I saw Martha's shocked face. As she pulled away from me my hand naturally grabbed the metal to pull her back to my embrace. I heard a loud humming sound and an electric shock traveled up my arm across my body and everything went black!

CHAPTER 8

I woke up with Logan laying beside me naked except for the ankh around her neck. We were in the bed in my hotel room and the last thing I had remembered was being in the luxurious bathroom about to step into the hot shower. Logan's hand was tenderly stroking my face. When she noticed my eyes roam her body she instinctively took the sheet and covered herself up to her chin. I could feel I was also naked beneath the blanket that covered me as well. My head felt very fuzzy as if I had been drugged. I didn't remember actually making love to Logan but I felt as if it had been in a dream. When I started to ask her what was going on and how long had I been laying there she said to just go back to sleep and she promised when we both had a chance to get a good night's sleep and feel refreshed she would explain everything in the morning. Hours later I awoke to an empty bed. I thought perhaps Logan was in the shower but when I went in she wasn't there. Next as I retrieved my robe from the bathroom floor I went into the lounge expecting to find her waiting for me. Instead I found a fresh pot of coffee and croissants and an envelope addressed to me.

Inside was this note:

> *Because I keep you in my heart and forever on my mind. You cannot go beyond my thoughts or leave my love behind. Our love is forever and our souls forever entwined. It is our Destiny!*
>
> *Till we meet again, L*

I called down to the desk, but they said since Logan had been my guest they did not know where or how to contact her. The waiter who had brought the tray of coffee up had said he had been given instructions to use the key and just leave the tray in the lounge. He did not see Logan leave. The bellman said he had flagged a cab for Logan but she did not give the cabbie a destination in front of him. He hadn't noticed anything else except that it was a yellow taxi. There were hundreds of taxis in New York City so without any other information finding Logan would be impossible. My only hope would be that she would pursue me just as she had before.

I didn't have too much time to lament on the disappearance of Logan as I needed to get to my next venue for my talk. As I stepped into the hot shower I remembered how beautiful Logan looked laying next to me in bed. Perhaps I should take a cold shower. I needed to bring my focus back to my speech and not on this mysterious woman.

I still didn't know her last name or anything about her. The shower felt wonderful. I needed to work out the kinks in my neck and back. I felt as if I had gone forty rounds in a boxing ring every part of my body ached. As I washed my body I noticed a faint bruise in the center of my chest. How had I gotten that I wondered. It was such a curious shape as well. I could barely make it out but it appeared to be a cross with an oblong circle at the top of it. It seemed familiar but right now I didn't have any spare time to ruminate where else I had seen that symbol before.

I quickly packed my bags and had the bellhop bring them down to the lobby where I checked out and had the doorman hail me a taxi to take me to Penn Station to catch a train to Philadelphia. It was a bright sunny day and the seven minute ride down Fifth Avenue was relatively quick. I had opened the cab's window to take in the cacophony of sights, sounds and smells: the hot dog vendors; the pushcart merchants selling their roasted chestnuts even in this August heat; the various street vendors with their makeshift tables covered in fake wristwatches and knock-off Armani and Coach purses. I got out as the cab triple parked outside Penn Station on 34th Street. I gave in to my urge for a hot pretzel from the corner cart. He was talking so fast I didn't realize what the purchase price was until in the time it would take to breathe in and out once he had given me the pretzel, plucked my $5 dollar bill from my hand and given me change back and was on to the next purchase. I could never get used to this fast pace of New York City. Even though London was quite a large city I never felt the need to quicken my step or rush my speech when dealing with a street merchant. Not even when at Victoria Station. The train information was quite easy to follow and even though there are always a multitude of people traveling through the station it seems less chaotic then Penn Station.

As I approached the long lines to purchase my train ticket to Philadelphia I realized just how big Penn Station really is. I resorted to asking the first police officer I saw which way it was to purchase an Amtrak ticket to Philadelphia. He looked me up and down. I believe he liked what he saw because he grinned and said in an Irish brogue that Philly would be richly blessed to have my company. I thanked him and after about ten minutes I found my way to the correct counter to purchase my ticket. The train would not be leaving for another hour and fifty minutes so I went in search of a place to have a quick bite to eat. I would save my jumbo pretzel for the train ride. My friend Kiernan had traveled to the States a few times and had given me a list of places I should go to if I had the chance. He had said Mc Sorley's Old Ale House on 7th and 3rd Ave was touted as New York City's Oldest Irish Pub. He said that they claim to have opened their doors in 1854 but there is some discrepancy about the actual date. He said that women were not allowed in Mc Sorley's until 1970. After the National Organization for Women filed a discrimination case against the bar, the bar was forced to admit women, but it did so very reluctantly. With the ruling allowing women to be served, the bathroom became unisex. Sixteen years later, a ladies room was installed. Kiernan said I would only be able to get either a light or dark beer, which would be fine by me. In the UK that would not be considered to be that old at all. Back home The Tipperary is the oldest Irish pub in London and celebrated its 400th anniversary in 2006. The pub dates back to 1605 but only became an Irish pub in 1700, and was possibly the first pub outside of Ireland to serve draught Guinness.

The Tipperary was called 'The Boar's Head' but changed its name after the First World War in a nod to the song 'It's a long way to Tipperary' which many regulars had sung in the trenches.

I did want to venture back to Greenwich Village but I wouldn't have time now. I decided to go to Tir Na Nog an Irish pub just across from Penn Station. I had noticed it when I stopped to get my pretzel. The cop who had directed me to the Amtrak counter with his Irish lilt of a voice got me thinking a nice pint would be good to quench my thirst. I fully intended to sleep when I got on the train later so a nice drink was in order.

As I entered the bar I decided to forgo sitting at the actual bar and instead opted for a small table towards the back wall. As I made my way through the throngs of tables the smell of wonderful food and ales greeted me. Although the music was quite loud I thoroughly would enjoy my meal listening to it. Before my bum was fully seated on the chair a waiter was at my side asking if I knew what I wanted to drink and eat. I decided rather than attempting to pursue the vast menu I would order a shepherd's pie and a shandy beer. True to his word the waiter came right back with my shandy. In a matter of minutes my shepherd's pie was set before me in a large deep dish. The crusted baked potatoes on top were toasted perfectly. As I delved beneath the potatoes the mixture of meat and vegetables were delicious. I saw I still had fifty minutes before the train would be boarding. As I was just about to order another Shandy, three woman approached my table. One of them had my book tucked under her arm. The tall redhead asked if I would mind signing my book for her. She said she was at last evening's lecture but the line had been too long for her to wait and she needed to relieve the babysitter. Responding to her by way of holding out my hand, she placed the book in my hand and the other woman stepped aside to make way for the waiter who asked if I needed anything further. Before I could say yes, I would like another beer, the blonde chick handed him a twenty dollar bill and said it was her treat. I then learned the redhead's name was Jane, her blonde-headed friend was Ruth, and the third woman was Susan. After handing the book back to Jane both Susan and Ruth pulled out books from their bags and asked if I wouldn't mind signing their books as well. Thankfully, the waiter appeared with my shandy and ushered the small group away saying that they should leave me now to enjoy the rest of my meal in peace. This waiter was definitely getting a bigger tip. Even though in England it is not customary to leave large tips (and sometimes not at all) I know in the States it is.

When he came to clear my plate he asked if I would like anything else, perhaps another drink, and I responded by saying if I had another drink I would not know what stop to get off in Philadelphia. He told me that I should get off near 1600 Arch Street at the other Tir Na Nog location.

He said they have a great happy hour and to ask for his friend Paddy Mac at the bar saying Patrick O sent me from New York. He told me Paddy Mac would take good care of me. I didn't know how far Archer Street was from the Marriott Hotel I was staying at, but I took the card he offered from his breast pocket with info on the back. As I walked back to Penn Station I realized that between the heat of the day and the two very strong shandy's I was a little tipsy. The fact that I hadn't slept well when I finally did go to bed with all the drama with Logan I was well and truly knackered. I had decided that I would definitely sleep on the train for the first hour at least. I would set my alarm on my phone to vibrate. That way I could get the lay of the train stations along the last leg of my journey.

As the Irish cop said, I would be on my way to Philly soon. I would take a taxi to the Marriot Hotel and then check my laptop for the person's info who would be meeting me in the morning for tomorrow's lecture. Normally, I would go over my notes again for the lecture, however, I felt it was best to gauge the room's knowledge and then proceed accordingly. The contact person for this event had stated that there would be approximately one hundred and fifty people in the audience so I would be able to give my talk on the paranormal and ghosts, then answer questions for the last twenty minutes. Since I basically lived my lecture on what it is like to live in a haunted house and communicate with those on the Other Side, it wasn't that I could forget the content of my talk.

I may, however, from time to time find myself being waylaid along my talk by one of those Spirits who like to have me share the spotlight with them. Therefore, I did have a format that I followed depending on how long each event was. Tomorrow's talk was from noon through a half past two o'clock with the last bit signing my books and taking pictures with the audience. I loved when I received copies of the photos that showed not only myself and the audience member but clear orbs that had wanted to get their picture taken as well. Sometimes it would be a relative of the audience member but mostly it would be one of my many helpers in the Spirit world. My Mum or Nana were regulars who would routinely interrupt my talk with tales they wanted me to recount from my childhood. No matter how many times I told them the audience was only interested if it was something extraordinary they would persist. Once when my Nana got a little testy with my ignoring her she decided to play with the hall's lighting making it flicker on and off. Then when the stagehand said not to worry it was only the old wiring she decided to shut the microphone off completely. Then when I still did not tell her story she shut the lights completely! When the audience gasped in surprise I decided I better tell the tale she wished. Thankfully, as I loudly proceeded to shout out the tale the microphone and the lights came back on. I learned from that experience not to ignore them, especially Nana.

Another time when I was giving my talk in an old theatre in France, after having finished the points I had wanted to make, I started to hear a violin playing. I thought it was the stagehand's system to segway into the question and answer period. As I started to take the first question the music became louder and louder. When I turned to the stagehand to ask them to please lower the music, he said he was not doing it and did not have violin music. Each time I would turn to the audience to answer another question the violin music became more pronounced and faster paced. This apparently was one insistent, musically gifted violinist who did not want to share the limelight with the likes of me.

I told the audience my thoughts about the violinist and proceeded in front of the audience to have a conversation with the dead violinist. He told me that he had been attempting to get everyone's attention by playing the violin but no one before me had the ability to hear what he had to say. They would just leave without him being heard. Of course the audience was only able to hear my side of the conversation. I summarized that he had been at the theatre late one evening practicing his violin for his upcoming solo act. The year was 1887 and it was a bone chilling evening.

He was finding it hard to play because his fingers would become too cold so he started a small fire in a steel drum that had been left just inside the back door. He used scraps of paper and old wooden timber he found out back. Unbeknown to him the steel drum had a residue that was highly flammable and when he lit the match the flame soared up higher than the brim and caught the curtain on fire. He did his best to put it out but the acrid smoke quickly had him gasping for air and he succumbed to the smoke. A large part of the theatre went up in flames and was destroyed. The concert he had longed to do had to be cancelled and his name was forever linked to ruining the Salle Favart Theatre. He simply had wanted to tell how he did not mean for it to be destroyed and he wanted people to hear him play. Well, he finally had his audience!

When he nodded that he was ready to play for us the piece he had composed especially for his solo concert, I had the stage manager put a spotlight on the center of the stage and lower the house lights. I asked the audience to please remain silent as we were to be honored to hear Monsieur Léopold

Aimon play this violin piece he composed for the very first time. I stepped to the side of the stage and nodded at Monsieur Aimon to indicate whenever he was ready. The music started off very soft and I felt it was done intentionally to draw you in to its rapture. I found myself moving my body as the melody seductively reached my ears. I began tapping my foot to the beat as it picked up its pace. Before long the entire audience was tapping along also. When he was done the audience leapt to their feet applauding and yelling "Bravo!" As I looked to center stage he materialized before us. I believe the EMF (Electronic Magnetic Frequency) generated by the clapping and foot tapping allowed him to use it to materialize. He had tears in his eyes as he looked over at me and bowed. I looked at the audience briefly and when I looked back to where he had stood; I saw just a small spark of light fly up into the ceiling of the theatre and disappear. He was now able to truly rest in peace, he was able to share his music and tell us he did not set the fire on purpose. Back when the fire happened and they found his body they theorized he set the fire on purpose because he was afraid to play his solo piece. There was talk that he was a drunk and that he no longer had the discipline to practice the violin the long hours required to be a fine musician. Tears started to stream down my face just then also. I was so happy to be of service in this way. His Spirit was no longer earthbound and tormented. I asked the audience to please give me fifteen minutes and then I would return to answer questions and stay to autograph my books. I needed to say a prayer of gratitude to God, my Angels and helpers in the Spirit world for my many blessings in being able to help lost souls.

When I returned to the stage a comfortable high backed chair and a table with a pitcher of water and a cup of tea were set up next to the microphone. There were three microphones set up in various parts of the theatre to allow people to queue up to ask their questions. Sometimes a person will ask a very personal question that will require me to tap into their soul family. When that happens I just needed to be curt and repeat that if they wanted a communication with their Loved Ones in Spirit they needed to make an appointment. Afterwards, the people who asked me to sign their book told me how fascinating it was to actually witness how it is done. As someone who was basically born talking to the Spirit world I did not see the uniqueness in it but I am grateful for it as it has become my bread and butter.

My first book was about being haunted by Sadie; a ghost who had lived and died in the cottage my family had bought when I was an infant. Sadie did not take well to the idea of sharing a home with another family. Although I now have a flat in London, I was actually born and raised in Belleek in County Fermanagh, Northern Ireland. Although the cottage was small by American standards, the four of us children - two boys and two girls - our parents and Nana lived there comfortably. We raised sheep and grew our own vegetables and although we weren't rich in material things I look back on those times with fond memories. We attended a small school during the week and on the weekends we were each expected to help with the chores. On Sunday we would dress for church and then gather at the Local afterwards. My Da & sometimes my Mum as well would have a pint and all the kids would gather and play Rings. No matter what age we were so long as we could throw the ring hoops towards the pegs on the wall we could play. The one with the most rings on the pegs wins. Or we would play Mr. Fox where one child is Mr. Fox and the other children line the wall. Mr. Fox stands about 10 feet away with his back turned. The children in the line say, "What time is it Mr. Fox?" He replies, "one o'clock." Then the children walk slowly toward the fox, repeating the question and answer until the Fox says, "Dinner time." The fox chases everyone back to the wall. If anyone is tagged, he/she is now the Fox. Another game we played was The Letter. We would sit in a circle with one child on the outside holding a crumpled piece of paper (the letter). This child walks around the outside of the circle while everyone sings with their eyes closed...

> *I sent a letter to my mother and on the way I dropped it. Someone must have picked it up and put it in their pocket.*

After the song, everyone looks behind them. The person with the letter behind them chases "it" back to the original seat. It is similar to the American game Duck, Duck, Goose.

Growing up listening to the grownups I knew I would want to travel and see the world. Mr. O' Shannesy from down the lane, had a daughter who had married a bloke from America and to hear him tell it, the streets of America were lined with Gold, especially New York City. Our own big cities in Ireland were never spoken of in such a wistful manner. In retrospect Belfast, Londonderry, and Omagh are just as lovely as those cities in America but with a much smaller population.

My first memories of Sadie, the original owner of the cottage we lived in, was waking up in my crib to a woman leaning over me singing. She had dark curly hair tucked under a bonnet with wisps framing the side of her face. I wasn't afraid even though she was not part of my family I knew. I looked over at my siblings in their beds and they were fast asleep. I wondered why this woman was singing to just me. Then she realized I had awakened and she started to shake my crib to and fro as my Mum would do. Within minutes I must have fallen back to sleep because when I opened my eyes later it was morning and everyone was moving about the cottage preparing for the day. The following evening she appeared again and when I stood up to call out for my Mum to get me, she rocked the crib again, started humming, and motioned for me to lay back down. I remember on and off throughout the time I was still in a crib she would appear and rock me back to sleep singing a tune I did not know. My Mum and Nana often would hum a tune to me as they fed me or rocked me to sleep but this was not one of those. As I got older and shared a bed with my siblings I would sometimes wake up to see her standing at the foot of our bed but she would not sing to me then.

One night I was alone in bed, being the youngest I would have to turn in earlier, she came to me before I fell asleep. I was only five years old then, and when I asked this kind woman her name she said to just call her Sadie. When I told my Da & Mum about a woman who sang to me they just said that it was nice I had someone else to care for me. I realized as an adult they thought I had an imaginary friend. Then, when I was old enough to tell them the woman's name I remember the shocked look on their faces. My Mum made the sign of the cross as she repeated the woman's name out loud to my Da as if she couldn't believe her own ears. Da looked at me and asked again for me to repeat the woman's name and to tell him what she looked like and what she did when she was with me. When I finished telling him, he also made the sign of the cross this time, which made me feel as if I had done something wrong. I started to cry then and my Da took me in his strong embrace and said not to fret, everything was okay, and he would take care of it. I wasn't quite sure what needed to be taken care of but I felt safe in Da's arms and stopped crying. Just then my siblings came in from outside and asked what was the matter. My Da whispered in my ear that it was our little secret. He said not to mention anything about Sadie but to come to him if she came back.

I felt very special that I had a secret, so I did as I was told. My brother John tried to get me to tell him by bribing me with a promise to show me what he had in his treasure box. His treasure box was an old cigar box that he kept behind the barn under the old rotted cart. On the very few and far between times when we were allowed to have a lolly from the general store, John would try and entice me to give him mine. He would always try to keep whatever he had and get as many of us to give him ours as well. As the oldest he would take full advantage of our naivety. My mother would sometimes catch him in the act and tell him to quit his malarkey and give the items back to us.

It was a very long time until I saw Sadie again. In hindsight, I believe it was because even though sometimes I was alone in my bedroom, my parents had one ear always on alert to see if Sadie would return. This particular time was after we had been at the Local and in the evening we went swimming down at the lake. We had all returned home knackered and I fell into a deep sleep. I awoke to that familiar humming. When I opened my eyes and looked around the room, Sadie was standing in the corner by the door. I sat up and before I could call out to my parents Sadie motioned for me to be silent. I whispered to her that I wanted to ask her some questions and if she was willing to answer them I would not call out to my parents.

She nodded her head and floated across to my bed and sat on the edge of it so I didn't have to shout to be heard.

My first question were who was she and why did she only come to me? She said I reminded her of her own daughter and that she once lived in this house. She said her husband had gone away and left her without knowing she was with child. He never returned. She got a wistful look in her eye when I asked her where her daughter was. She just told me her daughter's name was Mary Rose. Just then my sister entered the room and Sadie vanished. I raced from the room calling out for my Da. I leapt into his lap as he was sleeping on the sofa in the sitting room. Clearly I startled him because he let out a bad word my parents told us never to use. Once he saw it was me he apologized and asked what the matter was. I told him about Sadie's visit and his face grew paler.

He put me down saying we needed to tell Mummy. When we went into my parents' bedroom my mother was brushing her long beautiful hair. She turned startled to see me with Da, and at first she seemed annoyed to be interrupted. Da told me to repeat exactly what had happened. Once again my Mum made the sign of the cross as she blessed herself. In one quick move she took the crucifix off her wall above their bed and had me hold it to my chest and made the sign of the cross over me. I was more afraid of my Mum's reaction than I was of speaking to Sadie. Since my Mum had me clinging to her so tightly I realized she was wearing a very pretty sheer nightie and she smelled wonderful.

I was old enough to know that my parents were expecting it to be a night when we were told not to disturb them and that was probably why my Mum had the reaction to my presence at first. My Mum stood up then and told me to go back to bed now that my sister was with me and not to worry. I didn't understand why I would worry in the first place so this made me thoroughly frightened. When I went into my bedroom my sister was still awake and I had to tell her what was going on. I felt I would burst if I held it in any longer. Instead of making me feel safe and protected she told me to sleep the farthest I could from her and that I was daft in the head. She did not believe me at all. She said in all these years that I supposedly had Sadie coming to me she would have seen her, as well or at least heard her humming. She also said what was so special about me that Sadie would only come when I was alone. When I told her about reminding Sadie of her own daughter she said that was utter foolishness that I made up to feel special. In a huff she said for me to close my eyes and leave her be. This woman Sadie was turning out to be a real hornets' nest, no one seemed pleased to know about her being in our home with us.

The next morning I was just coming around the corner of the kitchen when I overheard my Mum & Da telling Nana about Sadie. I instinctively stepped back into the shadow so as not to be seen.

I especially wanted to hear what Nana had to say since she had lived in this house the longest. Nana said when she was a child she too would hear a woman's voice singing at night when she slept but she never saw her. When she was a little older and playing in the attic she found a babies blanket embroidered with the name Mary Rose on it. There were also little knitted dresses and booties as well. She took them down to her mother and asked if she could have them for her dollies. Her mother said she had never seen them before and that she would wash them carefully and after they were dry on the line she could have them back. Nana said she went about her day playing with the neighborhood children and forgot all about the items hanging on the line. After dinner when she went to bring the scraps out to turn over in the garden for mulch she noticed the clothesline was empty. When she asked her mother where the baby items were for her dolls her mother said she hadn't taken them down yet. Her father would never do woman's work but she asked him anyway. He laughed and said he didn't touch them to go back and ask her mother again. When Nana's mother said she hadn't seen or touched them again after pinning them up in the morning to dry; her father snickered and said it was probably that damn ghost again. Nana's mother told him not to start that foolishness again by speaking of the dead and he should let sleeping dogs lie. No one knew what had happened to the babies clothes until the following day. Nana went up into the attic to see if it might hold similar treasures. She was baffled when she opened the lid of the chest and found the freshly laundered babies clothes lovingly folded and covered in tissue paper.

She gathered them up and in her excitement she mustn't have seen that first step. She tumbled down the ladder and came crashing down. Her mother and father came running in to see what the commotion was and upon seeing the items in Nana's hands her mother screamed. She knew she hadn't put them up there. Her father was right it must be the ghost. Nana thankfully wasn't too bruised but she was warned never to touch that trunk again. Her father took the baby items from her and her mother refolded them and placed them away in the trunk once again.

Before Nana was born her own mother had been warned about a ghost who would be found standing over the newborns crib. She was told stories of how when the woman leaning over the crib was confronted she would vanish into thin air. The tale that was told to Nana's parents was that, before the troubles, a lad from the village had gone off to England and brought himself back a woman named Sadie. He built this cottage for their home and intended to make a life together for them there. Seamus was naïve in the ways of the world and particularly how the village closed ranks to shun the likes of that girl. Not only was Sadie a foreigner from the country they hated, but she was a Jew. She stood out like a sore thumb among the villagers. Shamus's parents disowned him and said they would never have anything to do with him as long as he was with her. As truth be told, Seamus didn't need further reasons to drink more than he had previously, for he was known to imbibe till he was found in the gutter sleeping it off. So it came as no surprise to anyone that one day he up and left once again. Sadie was beside herself with fear and sorrow. She hadn't gotten to know anyone at all, so she had no one to turn to.

Similarly, Sadie's own parents had disowned her. They had named her Sadie because that was exactly how they saw her, as their little princess. She knew her name meant princess and that she was always supposed to grown up to marry a nice Jew, preferably a Rabbi, to give them tons of grandchildren. Sadie's mother had been unable to carry any of her other pregnancies to full term, so Sadie was an only child.

When she met Seamus, with his carrot top hair and freckles, she fell madly in love. Sadie was so different from the lasses back home and the rebel in him gave him the courage to ask her out. Of course their romance was well hidden from the family and community. They made such an odd couple. He was tall and broad shouldered and swore like the sailor he was. She was petite, with dark curly hair and was very refined. Had she stayed she would have taught at the rabbinical school until marriage and her own children came along.

She and Seamus had been together less than a year when he left. Shortly after she found out she was pregnant. The child was illegitimate. Neither religion would accept their union so they had never married. The neighbor heard the cries the night Sadie was giving birth, and being a mother of seven herself, she ran over to help. When her husband told her not to get involved, she shushed him by saying to have another beer and stop being an arse. The girl was no more a babe herself she was going over to help.

Sadie was alone on the kitchen floor when Kathleen found her and it was a hard labour, all in all, but a beautiful little girl was born. When Kathleen asked Sadie what the child would be named. Sadie said she found herself praying to Mary their Blessed Mother. Seamus had bought a statue of Mary and placed her in their yard. She felt she needed a Mother's help and she was the one that came to mind. Since it was May she had seen her first rose open that very day so she added this name. Thus, Mary Rose was born. Sadie had spent the long lonely days prior to Mary Rose's birth knitting a blanket and booties and hats and sewing little nightgowns. Kathleen told her that was a fine name for a dear child. As she cut the umbilical cord, Kathleen said her own prayers for this wee child who had just been born to an unwed Jewish mother in a close knit Irish community. She would need all the help she could get. She cleaned up Sadie and the newborn as best she could and helped her to her bed. She told her she would return as soon as she was able and not to be frightened if it was late at night after her own little tikes were tucked in bed.

The money Seamus had left for Sadie hadn't been much, but between her vegetable garden and her few chickens, she and the baby had managed for the first few months. Sadie was nursing Mary Rose and the baby seemed to be doing well. Kathleen, a woman of her word, did manage to come in the evenings once every week or so and check up on them. She would bring over the few leftovers she would have from her own huge family's meals. Occasionally, Kathleen would bring a little dress or garment for Mary Rose that her own daughters had outgrown. Mary Rose was a mixture of her dad's coloring, with her blue eyes and tightly curled red hair and Sadie with her curved, predominant nose on that pink cheeked face. She was very petite. As the months passed, Kathleen noticed that Mary Rose was not growing as quickly as her own children had. She looked fragile and her complexion was sallow.

On one evening when Kathleen went to check on Sadie and Mary Rose she noticed that the wee lass was coughing something fierce. She sounded like a barking seal. Sadie was also pale and had the beginnings of the cough herself. Kathleen told her she should prop the baby up in her crib so as to allow her lungs to get a full breath. She took a clean rag and wet it and held it to the baby's forehead. Mary Rose's head was burning with fever. Kathleen knew that she could do no more for either of them, and that she had to leave before she too would be affected. This sickness had taken the lives of adults and children alike in the village before, and she knew it could spread to herself and her family. She told Sadie she would leave some food and a tonic at the door in the morning but that she would not be setting her foot upon the doorstep until they were better. True to her word she left a tonic of cod fish oil and cinnamon as well as some chicken broth the next morning. The following evening she went to leave some more food for Sadie and Mary Rose. When she turned the corner all she saw was the overturned pot licked clean, no doubt by the various cats that roamed the streets. The waxed paper had been torn apart as well. She knocked at the cottage door but there wasn't any answer. She prayed she would not find what she feared she would. She crossed herself and took her hanky out of her apron pocket and held it to her mouth as she turned the knob to enter the small cottage. It was stifling hot and eerily quiet. As she crossed the threshold of the bedroom she spotted them lying there. Sadie had Mary Rose clung to her chest in a death hold. Kathleen did not need to go up to them to feel for a pulse. The look on Sadie's ashen face spoke volumes. The only question Kathleen had was which one of them had passed on first. It didn't really matter now. They were both in God's hands.

Kathleen said a quick prayer for their souls and ran from the house. She went first to the barn and took a piece of coal and marked a big X across the door as a symbol to others to keep out. She didn't want others to catch this lethal cough. She found her husband plowing the fields and with a heavy heart she told him of their neighbors passing's. He wasn't surprised by the news after hearing his wife speak of the ills they had both had. Lots of villagers had passed from the consumption. She told him how she had marked the door even though Sadie never did get any company besides herself. Her husband remarked that Seamus would never know he had been a father for a little while anyway and it was just as well.

Because Sadie and Mary Rose had been infectious, they would forgo the typical wake of two nights sitting with them and no portions of the Scriptures would be read for this solemn occasion. No one knew or would be held to say a Jewish prayer. However they did place mother and child on a board on the floor where the spirit was thought to be in touch with the mysterious forces of the earth. Kathleen mixed a platter of salt that was mixed with earth and placed it on the stomachs of Sadie and Mary Rose. The salt was a symbol of the spirit; earth represented the flesh. With very little ceremony a few of the closest neighbors walked behind Kathleen and her family members to the village's church graveyard. They were sure to leave a good distance so as not to be infected as well. The priest looked over at Kathleen and asked who it was he was to say prayers for now.

Kathleen informed him it was their neighbor Sadie and her infant daughter Mary Rose. The priest asked what the Christian surname of the deceased was. Kathleen gasped audibly and started to shake her head as an indication that she did not know it. She realized that as far as she knew Seamus didn't marry Sadie before they arrived in the village. She crossed her fingers together behind her back and shot a warning look at her husband to say nothing. She said the first Irish Christian name that came to her head. With a bold look she blurted out the mother and child were the O'Shea's. She had heard of a family that lived on the outskirts of the neighboring village whose son was named Seamus and was a sailor. She didn't know if he was the actual father but it would have to make do for the purpose of having a decent burial for these two. The priest said the prayers over the shrouded bodies and afterwards everyone marched home out of the sweltering heat.

In the years following Sadie and Mary Rose's death every family that had moved into that cottage had experienced some sort of haunting. My Nana said her mother felt that the reason Sadie always was seen singing over a baby's crib was that she was protecting the child from harm. She wasn't able to save her own child from the consumption and she felt guilty.

We would never know what the true reason was for Sadie's careful watch but at least we now knew she meant no harm. I felt sad for Sadie and her infant daughter. As the years went by I would invite Sadie to sit with me in the evening and she would sing that familiar tune to me over and over again until I was lulled to sleep. Numi, numi. When I was old enough I found the translation to this song. It is:

Sleep, sleep, my little girl.
Sleep, sleep.
Sleep, sleep, my little one,
Sleep, sleep.

Daddy's gone to work -
He went, Daddy went.
He'll return when the moon comes out
-
He'll bring you a present!

Sleep, sleep...

Daddy went to the vineyards -
He went, Daddy went.
He'll return when the stars come out -
He'll bring you grapes!

Sleep, sleep...

Daddy went to the orchard -
He went, Daddy went.
He'll return in the evening with the
wind -
He'll bring an apple!

Sleep, sleep...

Daddy went to the field -
He went, Daddy went.
He'll come back in the evening with
the shadows -
He'll bring you ears of grain!

My audiences were always so fascinated by the tales I told about my numerous encounters with the Spirit world. My main reason for writing my first book was to let people know that this is quite common and that they should not be afraid of our Loved Ones in the Spirit world. It is as if they moved to a foreign country and they now speak a different language. You both need to be patient with one another and learn the technique that best works for you to communicate. What are you comfortable with? If you say you want your dead loved one to visit you in your home then don't be surprised when you come home from work and see their apparition at your kitchen table waiting with a cup of tea.

CHAPTER 9

The train ride to Philly was a restful journey for me. When I arrived at the station I found my way to the taxi stand and got in the queue. It wasn't too long a wait. Without intending on eavesdropping, I heard my name mentioned by two women who were a few people in line behind me. They were talking rather loudly. I gather so as to be heard over the din of all the traffic whizzing by. They mentioned how they were so excited to be able to see me in person after reading my books. Part of me, perhaps the ego, wanted to step out of line and address them and tell them I was happy they had made the decision to go to my lecture.

As I was having this debate with myself, my taxi pulled up and the driver got out to put my luggage in the boot. Just then, the one woman recognized me from my picture on the jacket cover of my book she was holding. She yelled out my name, so I turned in their direction and I nodded and waved in acknowledgement as I climbed into the taxi. Well, if this was any indication of the reception I was to receive tomorrow it should be a lovely afternoon.

The driver asked where to and I replied the Marriott please, as I leaned forward and handed him the address in that little window. As we pulled up to the Marriott, a doorman came around and opened the door and retrieved the luggage the taxi driver took out of the boot. I paid the taxi driver giving him what I hoped was a nice tip and followed the doorman inside. Another gentleman took the luggage from the doorman who tipped his hat and told me to have a good stay. Than the new man rolled my luggage on a brass luggage trolley across the huge expanse of the lobby to the front desk. I gave the receptionist my name and confirmed the two days of my stay and took out my credit card for miscellaneous things I may wish to add. The room had been prepaid by the group I was lecturing at tomorrow. I was led up to my room by a different bell hop who opened the door for me, placed my luggage on the rack and smaller case on the bed, and asked if there was anything else he could do to make my stay more enjoyable to let him know. I tipped him as well and said I would let him know as I closed and locked the door behind him.

I think Larry, as his name tag read, could get me just about anything at all I may be wanting, legal or not, was what my intuition told me. Well other than the occasional drink I did not take drugs. Therefore, I could not think of any other services Larry could provide me. I turned on the telly for background noise as I made my way around the room unpacking my toiletries and clothes. As the last bit was put away I noticed a lilac colored envelope had been slid under the doorsill. I bent to retrieve it and as I did so, I heard my Nana's voice in my left ear whisper, "Be careful dearie, all is not what it seems!"

Oh boy! Never one to mince words, Nana was being a bit mysterious herself. Instead of just telling me what she meant I left the envelope where it lay and went to my suitcase and pulled out my sage and crystals. Before I did anything else I would cleanse and bless this room and set my intentions for my stay here. As I stood by the door to the room I lit the white sage and uttered these words,

> *Bless this dwelling, O' Lord I pray,*
> *make it safe by night and day;*
> *Bless these walls, so firm and stout keep*
> *want and trouble out;*
> *Bless the roof and chimney tall, let thy*
> *peace lie over all;*
> *Bless the door that it may prove ever*
> *open to joy and love;*
> *Bless these windows, shining bright,*
> *letting in God's heavenly light;*
> *Bless everyone who walks within, keep*
> *them healthy and may they find peace*
> *within.*
> *Amen.*

I walked about left circling to the right being mindful to get each corner.

Hotel rooms in and of themselves are a bevy of activity of emotions being stored from previous living guests, not to mention Spirits who may roam the halls as well. I always bring my sage and crystals to form a space of protection for me. As I made my way back to the hotel door I extinguished the sage and put the crystals in my pocket as I bent to pick up the envelope. As I opened it I got a whiff of a particular perfume I had recently been introduced too. Now I knew why Nana said what she did. Without looking at the words I knew this had been written by Logan. I also thought how glad I was to remember to do this cleansing ritual. I clearly had not had the opportunity in New York and that stay was certainly chaotic!

The heady perfume scent was a mixture of sweet pea and an Egyptian oil. Once again I questioned how this woman had tracked me down to this hotel when I did not even know her last name. Before I read what she had to say, I went to the small fridge to see if they had the customary bottles of liquor. After placing a few cubes of ice in a tumbler I poured the bottle of Grand Mariner over it. I kicked off my shoes and tucked them beneath me in the oversized chair. Once I was settled in I opened the envelope again and read the letter.

> *My Beloved,*
>
> *I'm sorry to have disappeared on you once again. I know you have more questions than answers and I will answer them all in due time. Your itinerary says that you are giving a talk*

*at the Widener Lecture Room at the
University tomorrow. Although I would
love to be there I think it best I leave
you to concentrate on your lecture.*

*Afterwards, I will be waiting for you at
the Egyptian Gallery on the first floor
near the Sphinx.*

*Till tomorrow, sweet dreams (hopefully
of me)*

L

I re-read the letter and took another sip of my
drink. She addresses me as her beloved. Well right
off the bat she has fantasized our one-night-stand
to something it is not. Clearly, if I do see her again
I will have to set her straight. Even though she
shared my bed I have no recollection of actually
having it off with her. I do remember her kisses.
Especially her first bold kiss when she was waiting
for me outside the lecture hall in Manhattan. I did
wind up snogging it off with her right there while
Sharon looked on aghast. My tongue willingly
found hers.

Logan really did know how to keep me guessing. I
actually had planned on visiting the Egyptian
Gallery after my lecture. Now I would definitely be
checking it out. This probably would be the most

extraordinary museum visit I would ever have. As I sat nursing my drink I thought to myself that I most likely would be dreaming of Logan. With that, I got up, crossed the room and got prepared for bed. I made myself one more drink and placed it on the nightstand as I read from the hotels *Where To* magazine.

It said that the Sphinx Gallery houses one of the finest collections of Egyptian architecture on display in the United States. A 15-ton red granite sphinx, the largest in the Western Hemisphere, dominates the gallery. There is also a display of materials from the beginnings of Egyptian history and of a unified country of Upper and Lower Egypt, and some of the earliest hieroglyphs found in Egypt, dating from more than 5,000 years ago.

The magazine showed pictures of the Mummies Gallery with displays of carved reliefs, stone coffins, and three-dimensional sculptures. I was interested in seeing the human and animal mummies, tomb artifacts, and funerary objects and materials used in the mummification process. I had read about the Egyptian belief in an afterlife, and the complex funerary practices they developed over thousands of years.

I have been many times to the British Museum to see their vast displays of Egyptian culture and I it always felt so familiar.

I had always had a fascination with the afterlife, obviously, but anything and everything Egyptian I was always interested in finding out more about. I had several statues of Egyptian gods and goddesses. My favorite is Isis. I also have miniature pyramids and the eye of Horus. It would be wonderful to see actual statues and artifacts. Tomorrow promised to be a day of mysteries revealed. I took the last bit of my drink and turned off the light. As I said my nightly prayers, I thanked God for my many blessings and promptly fell into a deep sleep.

I saw myself standing on the Temple steps speaking to a throng of my people. They were frightened about the Syrian army's onslaught. They were looking to me as overseer to give them reassurances my father, the King, would protect them. They were raising their fists in anger and I feared for my very life. When they started throwing stones, I was whisked away from the melee by one of the priests. We ran through the Temple, chased by the angry mob. They also want me to release the grain that was stored in the pharaoh's warehouses. We were in a drought that was causing widespread famine. Although I felt for the plight of my people, my father would not budge on his decree to not only keep the grain that was currently his, he ordered me to collect a higher amount from each farmer who was already suffering. As I ran through the cavernous underground tunnels I prayed to Ra that I live to see another day.

BUZZZ Buzz Buzz my alarm clock sounded. I awoke from a fitful night's sleep. Now that wasn't very peaceful at all, I thought. Why did I dream that? I called down for a light breakfast to be sent up, preferring to ease into my day. I had plenty of time before my lecture and I thought I may use the time to go over my notes as well as meditate. If I was to meet Logan afterwards I needed to ground myself. For whatever reason this mysterious woman had a hold on me I wished to figure out. On the one hand, I don't remember ever having met her prior to yesterday's event in New York. However, she was so familiar to me in other ways. When she tilted her head a certain way, or gave me that smirk it tore at the edges of my memory. Later this afternoon I would have lots of questions that I was determined to get some logical answers too.

Breakfast was delivered, and after a cup or two of tea and a scone I got my clothes out for the day. After a nice shower, I dressed for my talk and walked to the lift. I had the piece of paper with my contact's name and information in my pocket. I walked out to the curb where the doorman hailed me a cab. I told the driver the name of the lecture hall and we proceeded to weave our way through heavy traffic till we got to the University. It normally was only a seven minute drive but there was an accident on John F. Kennedy Boulevard, the driver informed me. He weaved around and eventually we were on Walnut Street in front of the correct building of the University. I paid the driver, collected my briefcase and bag from the seat next to me, and walked up the front steps.

As I entered the front door I was greeted by a young woman holding out her hand to me in greeting. She introduced herself as Rebecca, my host for the afternoon's lecture. She asked if she should call me by my nickname, Alex, or did I prefer to be addressed in a different manner. I told her Alex was just fine. She offered to carry my briefcase, for which I was grateful. Although the places I lecture in order my books ahead of time, for the book signings, I always have my original copies with me to reference, and they can be quite heavy at times. As we came around the corner of the hallway I half expected to see Logan there, even though she said she would not be meeting me till afterwards. If truth be told I wished she was there with that same greeting she had provided me the last time we met.

My mind must have wandered for a moment and I realized Rebecca was holding the door to the lecture room open for me asking if the room would be okay. As I looked around the beautiful hardwood floors, balcony seating and massive stage I told her it was perfect. It would provide an ideal setting for my lecture. On the stage there were two comfortable chairs with a table between them. There was a beautiful bouquet of flowers in a lovely deep purple vase and a water pitcher and tumblers. Near the front of the stage a rectangular table was set up with my books for the autograph session afterwards. Rebecca pointed out a door to the left where there was a private powder room if I needed it. This girl was very in tune with my needs, for next she asked if she could bring me a cup of English breakfast tea. I laughed and said if she had Irish breakfast tea that would be better. Rebecca's face flushed just then. I told her either tea would do just fine and if she could put in a spoonful of honey it would be dandy.

When Rebecca arrived with my tea and honey I raised my cup and said cheers. The lecture room doors would be opening soon and I could hear a bevy of activity out in the hallway we had come through earlier. People were queuing up, for the best seats perhaps. I decided before they opened the doors I would visit the loo and do a little sprucing up. I also needed to put the microphone pack on that Rebecca had given me and affix the receiver to my shirt front.

Afterwards I stood off stage where Rebecca had showed me to wait while she introduced me. It took just a wee bit till the seats were almost full, and as the lights dimmed I said a prayer and called on my Angels and guides and those on The Other Side who had something to add to today's talk. Before I even finished I could feel the air change around me, growing thicker with their energy and I whispered a humbled welcoming greeting to my helpers.

Rebecca stood just then and turned towards me indicating she would announce me momentarily and I nodded my readiness. I pushed the button to turn the mic on. She also turned on her mic and proceeded to introduce me and invite me to join her on stage. As I came out from the corner the audience stood and clapped in anticipation of my talk. I motioned for them to take their seats as I took my own seat. This was to be in an interview style chat. Rebecca had previously sent me some of the questions she would be asking and then it would be opened to the audience for the last twenty minutes. Then we would have a ten minute break to allow me to visit the loo, freshen up, and perhaps have a fresh cuppa.

After doing twenty or so of this type of book interview I pretty much knew the flow and type of questions I would be asked. So I was tremendously surprised when the first question Rebecca asked was, "Why do you feel so many people resonate with Egypt? Could we all be reincarnated from that period and part of the world?" I must have looked thick as a plank because I didn't quite know how to answer that after last night's bad dream. Or was it a dream? It felt like a memory, I thought. My answer to Rebecca was more factual than knowing. I said that Egyptian culture is 5,000 years old so it stood to reason many people would have derived from that civilization. She asked what my own recollection of that lifetime was, if indeed I recalled one. As I looked out over the audience's expectant faces I heard my own guide whisper to me to tell what I remembered from last evening and more would come. That I should not be afeard of looking like an idiot. As I have learned over again and again it is useless to not listen to my guides. No good could come of it. He assured me it would not go all to pot. So, as I recalled last evening in vivid detail I did see it in my mind's eye as if it was on a movie screen. I am able to see things in this way even with my eyes open. I told about the throng of people, my people, demanding I do something for them. They needed the stores of wheat and grain to feed their families. Their angered voices echoed in my head as I heard Rebecca ask me if I knew what my name was and to describe my lifetime in Egypt. Without even consciously knowing I did it, I stood bolt upright and placed my right hand to the left side of my chest and then flung it straight out and up and announced, "I am Malachite, Overseer of the people."

There was an audible gasp from the audience that broke whatever spell I had just been in and I sat down. Rebecca didn't miss a beat by asking, "Malachite please tell us about your life." I spoke of the famine and the hard life of my people. I spoke of the sorrow I saw as a warrior in battle against the Syrians. I told of how I did not agree that my father the King should have many wives and that I was only one of his many children. I talked about the priests and priestesses of the Temple and how I loved to learn at the feet of the Scribes.

I spoke about how I was asked to betray my own father and when I refused I was held captive until the priests arranged a bribe. After my release, I was hidden among the peasant families that knew I always did what I was able to for them.

Before being driven from my own country I met a woman who I was enchanted with. She was seven years my junior. I learned that she had been taken captive from her home in Syria as a very young girl. She escaped and had lived on the streets until a farmer noticed her attempting to steal the feed he was giving his cattle. He had described her as a fierce little mite. She was only five when he and his wife took her in to live with his family. The farmer named her Raja which means hope. She agreed to go with me if the priests could arrange our passage aboard a ship to cross the Mediterranean into Jerusalem.

At that moment a mobile phone in the audience started to play loud music. It took me right out of that memory back to the present time, sitting on stage with my host Rebecca asking me questions. I must have looked as dazed as I felt because she then said that we would take a ten minute break. She reminded everyone to turn off their cell phones. When she turned towards me she asked me to follow her backstage. Once we were out of earshot of the audience she asked if I was feeling alright and could she get me anything. Actually, now that she mentioned it I was a bit woozy, so I took a seat in the grey steel folding chair she held out for me. I told her a cup of tea would be lovely if we had time. She said the audience would wait and talk among themselves till I was ready. When she left to get me my tea I sat with my head between my knees and then took a few deep breathes in and out till I felt more clear headed.

When Rebecca returned with my tea and some biscuits she asked me how we should proceed with the interview. I told her to please stick to the questions that she had previously sent me and not to ask any more questions about Egypt. She agreed and I stood and said I would bring my tea back over to the table and we could continue. When I returned, the audience immediately settled down and returned to their seats. For the next hour Rebecca asked only about things that were previously approved by me or were things pertaining to one of my books. Since we had already taken a fifteen minute break we dismissed that and went right into allowing the audience to ask questions for the remaining twenty minutes. The questions were pretty routine until a fellow from the back asked me about my life as Malachite. He wanted to know what my life was like after Raja and I fled to Jerusalem, were we happy there? For an instant I saw Raja's face clearly in my mind. She stood shoulders below mine and she was slight in stature. I could easily pick her up in my arms and I often did. Her hair was soft and had a sheen to it. It was black as the night sky. Her olive skin was soft but her body was strong. Although I was a warrior and had had many battles in the field I would easily have chosen to be in another rather than face my beloved's fury when she was angry with me. I heard myself echoing these things out loud but heard them as if someone else was saying them, if that made any sense.

The next woman asking a question wanted to know if we are a man in this life aren't we a man in all our reincarnations and vice versa? I replied, "Gads No! We return as either for whatever our destiny determines our path to be for each lifetime."

Rebecca stood up and thanked me for coming and announced I would be staying afterwards to autograph books for anyone who wished to purchase them. I would be there for a half hour longer. The audience stood and clapped for me. Rebecca turned off her own microphone, touched my elbow, and leaned in to whisper that if I was ready I could start signing then or if I needed the loo she would have them line up nicely and wait till my return. I told her I was fine and ready to begin signing. I reached under my jacket and behind my back and unclipped the microphone and handed the equipment to her. When I was seated in front of the book table I had two lines form. One of them had already purchased the book and just needed it signed and the other line was still waiting to receive their copy. I love order so I was quite pleased. The two women who I had overheard talking about me when I was getting into a taxi to go to the Marriott were simply beaming that I had waved to them when I first arrived. They were the first two on line. I find many people that have read my books feel I am their best chum without ever having met me before. On the one hand it is a true compliment and I treat it as such but then some people take it too far and become too close for my liking. They are touchy-feely and want me to come out with them or invite me to their homes and seem insulted when I decline.

After signing books and having to stop and take some photos with the audience and Rebecca I was free to leave. Rebecca said she would love to take me to dinner or at least buy me a drink to thank me. I didn't want to tell her I was already meeting Logan in the Sphinx gallery but there was no other polite way to get out of it. I needed to go in the opposite direction towards the lift, not follow her out the front door. When I told Rebecca I was already meeting someone she looked deflated. She said I was going to love the Gallery and to enjoy my time there. She also took out her card with her info on it and asked me to call her if I ever was back in Philly. She said she found me fascinating and she would love to get to know me better. With that she leaned in and kissed me on the cheek and bid me a good evening.

There was a restroom next to the bank of lifts so I went in to freshen up and compose myself for my meeting with Logan. Just thinking of seeing her again made my heart leap and other parts of me respond to the thought. I washed my face and combed my hair and took one more look in the long mirror as I exited the restroom. The image that I saw there met with my own approval. I had picked up a map to direct myself to where the Lower Egyptian Sphinx Gallery was, but I really did not need to refer to it. The building was well laid out and marked clearly.

As I got off the lift, I was to walk straight ahead towards the Rainey Auditorium and turn right and then the door leading to the Egyptian Gallery would be on my left. I showed the guard the ID card Rebecca had given me to gain access to the building, which eliminated the entrance fee. I was free to roam about all the galleries. On the third floor were the Egyptian mummies and other artifacts but since it was almost time to meet Logan I entered the designated room. My eyes were drawn straight ahead to the magnificent fifteen ton red granite Sphinx. Surrounding it are the gateway, columns, doorways and windows from the best preserved royal palace ever excavated in Egypt. The palace was built for the New Kingdom pharaoh Merenptah (r. 1213-1204 BCE) at the city of Memphis in Lower Egypt.

Upon seeing the Sphinx I felt I wanted to kneel before it in adulation but I was afraid of what others may think. Tears sprung to my eyes unbidden. I was overwhelmed with such emotion I openly started bawling. As I moved closer to the Sphinx an arm came around my waist and I breathed in Logan's scent. She said nothing then, she just held me as I cried. So much for looking my best, I thought as I opened my tear stained eyes. When I composed myself a little better I turned to face her. I was speechless! She took my breath away! She stood before me dressed in full women's

Egyptian apparel. She wore a long sleeveless white dress with a gold embroidered thick belt. The dress fell just above her gold ankle sandals. She wore gold ornate armbands and wrist cuffs that were connected to the cape around her shoulders. Her hair was now straight and dark as the night, and she wore an ornate gold headdress with beads. In the center of this headdress was a serpent with green eyes and a red tongue sticking out of its mouth. The elaborate neckpiece was covered in sparkling jewels and Egyptian symbols. Just below the neckline was the ankh she had previously worn when we first met. As I looked once again to study her face she smiled at me with that same twinkle in her green eyes.

She tilted her head to one side, leaned forward and kissed me. Logan then looked so deep into my eyes that I could see my own reflection in hers as she whispered to me, "Ana baḥibbak." In that instant hearing those words again I knew how this mysterious woman knew so much about me. She was my beloved, my Raja. It all made sense now. I took her in my arms and uttered the words I had spoken to her many lifetimes ago. First I said them in Arabic, "Ana baḥibbik," then in English, "I love you!"

We had held and kissed each other fervently for what seemed like forever until we noticed the lights flickering and heard the announcement the gallery would be closing soon and to please make our way to the exit. What next? I thought. I had all these questions and no answers, but all I wanted was to hold Logan, or should I call her Raja, forever. The reality was too extraordinary to even comprehend. How was it possible that she would be in my life again now? The dream I had last evening was a recollection of our lifetime together in Egypt. What I had recalled earlier in the lecture hall was preparing me for this moment. She reached for my hand and said to follow her. As she turned the corner she read my thoughts and said to call her Logan for that is who she is in this incarnation.

My legs were wobbly as we came through a rear doorway exit. It was now just after 5 pm and after being in the darkly lit gallery it took a few moments for my eyes to adjust. I was still holding Logan's hand as we entered the parking facility. She pointed to a red Audi convertible. Before getting into the driver's seat she asked me if I wanted to drive her car. I told her I did not even trust myself to make a coherent sentence much less navigate on the opposite side of the road than I was used to. I threw my suitcase in the backseat and got in the passenger side. As she put the car in gear she looked over and gave me a familiar smirk as she said, "Buckle up, you're in for the ride of your life!" I didn't doubt that for one minute.

When she got on what I felt was the outskirts of the city she pressed a button to make the top come down on the car. It slid nicely and quietly into a spot behind the rear seat. Now Logan kicked it into high gear and the wind caught her cape and it flew out behind her. Her hair danced in the wind and she was transformed into a carefree spirit. I was mesmerized by her. I did not understand what was occurring to us then but I literally was along for the ride. I fully intended to enjoy every precious moment of it.

The next book in the

Destiny of Lovers series

Love is Eternal

by Arlene Michel Rich

turn the page for a preview of

Love is Eternal....

CHAPTER 1

I gingerly opened my eyes to the piercing sunlight that was streaming in the opened barn door. I felt like someone had tied me to a horse and dragged me across a field. Every bone in my body hurt. When I sat up I noticed on my bare chest there was a scorch mark in the middle, as if I had been branded. It was in an odd shape with a cross that had a loop where the top line should be. I could feel the heat coming from it. My skin was hot to the touch but only in that area! I felt as if I had drank some of Mr. Stabler's special whiskey. But I hadn't touched another drop after the day when I had asked Mr. Stabler for Martha's hand in marriage.

The last thing I remembered was Sarah showing up unannounced at the barn door wearing only that flimsy nightgown. My resolve to stay true to Martha, went right out of my mind the minute Sarah removed her nightgown and knelt down naked and opened my britches.

I had not been with Sarah, in that way, for over six months. Six very long months.

Six months earlier, I had asked Martha to marry me and my father had died that very same day. What should have been a wonderful happy time had changed in the blink of an eye with his passing. As the only son I was now in charge of the general store. Even though my father and I did not agree on many things, I still missed him. People had relied on the fact that they could get all their supplies in one place. People came from many towns away to order their goods in Alexandria. I had never wanted to take over the running of the general store. I had many arguments with my father on that point. Thankfully, grandfather had left me this wonderful piece of land I could farm. All I ever wanted to do was to be a farmer. I loved when you planted a seed the land repaid you by growing crops. I had so far carefully tilled the land with the plow I had recently bought. He thought how after he finished building the home he and Martha would live in, he would be able to devote all of his time to planting his crops. The wedding was just a few weeks from now. Matthew lay there in the make shift bed he had been using while building the furniture and his home.

He remembered making love to Sarah but then Martha's face would come into his mind, then Sarah's. He didn't know whether it was his own guilt at having betrayed Martha, with laying with Sarah again, or if he was somehow dreaming all this. As he stood up his head was woozy and he grabbed the post to steady himself. There on the post, was a note nailed into the beam. It was from Martha and it said.

"I thought I would surprise you and bring you some supper. Luke had told me you weren't feeling well. I found you sound asleep. I intended to touch your forehead and see if you had a fever. You kissed me in a way you had never before and imagine my surprise when you started to take liberties by opening my bodice and grabbing at my breasts. You pulled at my chain and medallion and then you passed out again.

I can only assume you had been drinking my father's whiskey again. I thought you vowed off drinking whiskey. Our wedding night will come soon enough. Until then I thank you to treat me with the respect a lady is due. Love Martha"

Matthew knew then what had happened. After coupling with Sarah he must have fallen asleep and then thought Sarah had come back for more. She was insatiable most of the time and it was not unusual for her to totally wear him out. Without realizing it was Martha, his body responded with its usual need. No wonder he kept mixing up the two women in his thoughts.

Had it only been 2 years since Sarah came to live with his family and work in the store? Sarah had shown up one winter's night with just a satchel and a letter of introduction from her uncle James Monroe of Oak Hill, Virginia.

The Monroe family had known our family for generations and Sarah had wished to find employment in a more populated town. In his letter to my father he said his niece was of a adventurous spirit and would need to have her reigns tightened at times. He thanked my father for taking her into his employ. Sarah was my sister's age which made her two years my senior.

It had all begun that hot summer night when I tiptoed past Sarah's door only to discover she was sleeping totally naked. I had never lain with a woman before. The things Sarah did that night I became a man were etched in my memory and in every cell of my body. I was like putty in her hands and she always left me wanting more. Our secret times together were so amazing but I knew they would have to end. I had been very up front with Sarah from that very first time, I always intended to marry Martha. She seemed ok with it until that fateful day I announced in the store to my parents and Martha's parents, the Stabler's, that I was off to ask Martha in earnest. Sarah had run from the store with her hand over her mouth crying.

www.ingramcontent.com/pod-product-compliance
Lightning Source LLC
Chambersburg PA
CBHW071302130626
46556CB00003B/1429